MIDNIGHT REVELATION

"Well," cried Pete Reeve, "they were lies that I've told you. Want to know the straight of what I am? Want to know it?"

Bull stood up slowly, an enormous, imposing figure in the shadows.

"I've been a man-killer, Bull," continued the shrill-voiced little man in a frenzy of grief and self-accusation such as comes to everyone now and then, "just the way The Ghost has been a cattle-killer. And I've robbed and stolen, and fought other men for money I didn't have no right to. That's the truth about me, and if it was ever known they could hang me ten times for what I've done. There's the truth. And now get out and leave me. Go your way, and I'll go mine!"

He had expected an outburst of emotion; the calm of the big man stunned him.

"Why, Pete, if it's that way, it looks to me like you had more need of me than ever."

Pete Reeve gasped and choked. "You mean that, Bull?" he whispered. "You mean that?"

"You and me being partners," said Bull slowly, "of course I mean it."

MAX BRAND

BULL HUNTER'S ROMANCE

LEISURE BOOKS **NEW YORK CITY**

A LEISURE BOOK®

August 1996

Published by special arrangement with Golden West
Literary Agency.

Dorchester Publishing Co., Inc.
276 Fifth Avenue
New York, NY 10001

Printed in the United States of America.

BULL HUNTER'S ROMANCE

BULL HUNTER'S ROMANCE

CHAPTER I

TO SATISFY SPECULATION

THERE were three points of stategic interest, each ignorant of the one behind, because the rolling of the hills shortened every viewpoint, and the sense of smell was made useless by a strong, steady wind out of the east.

First there was a big, red bull who in the pride of his strength had wandered far from his herd; and second was a gray figure skulking from bush to rock; and third was a medley of mounted men trailing a pack of huge wolfhounds up the wind. But all were in a due line from east to west, and while the hounds knew vaguely of that distant gray figure, that ghostly thing itself could not use the trigger-balanced sense of smell, and was aware only of the lordly bull.

The latter wandered idly. He had already taken his fill of the grass of the late spring, grass that had sleeked his ribs and layered him with fat; now he strolled from titbit to titbit of the longest, darkest grass, and, having licked up a tuft of it, he went on again.

The gray stalker had observed him, now from a bush, now from a rock, as he glided, shadowlike, his body close to the ground. He was that fleetest of all the things that run on four feet in the Western mountains—fleetest and most enduring. The deer which might dart away from him in the opening spurt he would run to death in a few scant minutes; a greyhound might possibly—though it is doubtful—outsprint him, or a wolfhound, in fine trim, might outdistance him in the short run; but in ten minutes of ardent going he would break the heart of the fleetest dog that ever stepped. He had more than speed under foot. Of all the wild creatures that kill beneath the sky he was the wisest; the solemn old grizzly, lord of cattle-killers, compared to him, was blunt of wit, and the cleverest fox that ever ran was simply an impish child compared to the almost human brain of this mountain-runner.

In a word, he was that king of the wolves, the great, gray lobo. The State would pay fifty dollars for his scalp; and the ranchmen would double, treble, quadruple the price. Indeed, there was no price they would not pay for his head, for the lobo prefers hot meat; he kills before he dines, and after he dines he leaves his kill. For this particular animal, the despairing ranchers had littered the country with traps and scoured the mountains and the plains with wolfhound packs and fast horses. But they never had come within shooting distance. He seemed to know the exact range and capabilities of a rifle in expert hands, and when the sun sank and the treacherous light of the evening began, more than one hunter had seen the skulker running impudently close across the hills, a great, pale-gray, smoothly gliding form, and for that reason they called him "The Ghost."

A very palpable ghost, one would say, following the footprints, well nigh as large as a man's hand, to the rock behind which he had sunk to take another and a deliberate view of the bull. The lobo is the hugest of wolves, perhaps, and The Ghost was a giant of his kind. Indeed, he differed from the ordinary wolf in many ways. He had, to be sure, the lobo's gray pelt; he had the bushy tail and the long-snouted head, a broad head more bearish than doglike in full face, but sinisterly pointed in profile.

It was by looking at The Ghost in full face that one was aware of his distinctive features most accurately. He had the black lines like brows above his light-brown eyes, lines that gave him a whimsical, inquisitive look typical of his dreaded kind; but an expert would have noted that the head was excessively broad, and the forehead most unusually high, and the eyes large beyond precedent. His pelt, too, was less than wolfishly rough; it promised to be pleasant to the touch, and where the wind parted the outer coat one saw a silken inner lining. This in connection with the peculiarities of the head.

But what was it that was so different? Why was it that a man could look close at The Ghost without the chill that strikes into one's blood when one sees a true wolf, even behind the bars of a menagerie cage? All the differences, all the peculiarities, could be covered with a single phrase—there was something of the dog about The Ghost.

He sat down behind the rock, and opening his great mouth, grinned at the bull; that grin was all wolf. But now, as some distant sound came down the wind, and he pricked one ear and canted his head to listen—that was certainly the bay of a dog.

Now, as the bull sauntered away with a swishing of his tail, The Ghost slid from behind the rock, all wolf now. No dog since the beginning of time could have glided so shadowlike, his body trailing the grass, his shoulders low, his forepaws slipping out, one by one, with incredible softness. And the twitching lips that exposed the murderous long fangs—yes, he was all wolf now, and a strong man, a hunter, gun in hand, would have felt his skin prickle at the sight of him.

The bull had raised his head to look into the teeth of the wind. The moment his head went up, The Ghost was at him, a gray blur shooting noiselessly along the ground. He swept in a semicircle, edging toward the side from which the red bull had turned his head, and cutting in at the angle, he snapped as he shot by. It was like the slash of two heavy, keen sabers. The bull, with a bellow, started to turn; before the bellow was half uttered, before he had hobbled halfway around, the silent savage had checked himself and leaped back in the other direction, slashing the other hind leg. Completely hamstrung, the bull's quarters slumped heavily to the ground. He raised his forequarters, roaring with pain, pawing, tossing his head and those terrible horns. But there was no hope for him now. The lobo could sink his teeth with impunity into the flank of his victim and wait for him to bleed to death.

But that, oddly enough, was not the plan of The Ghost.

He slipped around until he stood face to face with the bull. It brought a fresh paroxysm of pain and terror and rage from the red giant. Even the lofty form of The Ghost, compared to the high-humped bulk of the red bull, was a slight thing. It seemed impossible that the one could have felled the other.

But The Ghost, having done his terrible work with such neatness, now seemed to relapse once more into the innocent, close student of nature. He licked the blood from his lips, and with the most meticulous care he cleansed a few random drops from the apron of white fur across his breast.

The bull, with much heaving and writhing, had worked himself around until he directly faced his antagonist. He had a mighty heart, had that red bull. His scarred front bore witness to many a battle with his peers from which he had emerged victorious, lord of his ranges. Now he shook his wide-spreading horns and bellowed defiance. Woe to the strongest lobo that ever lived, if it dared a face-to-face encounter with those horns. He knew the exact side-flourish which would drive the stout points through hide and bones and flesh and pin the murderer to the earth.

But further violence seemed infinitely far from the mind of The Ghost. He lay stretched out at ease, watching, waiting, with his big, gentle, brown eyes dwelling steadily on his victim.

That immobility on his side lasted for several minutes. Perhaps the bull began actually to doubt that this quiet creature could have been his assailant. At any rate, he raised his big head high and turned it to look down the wind. Far off, topping a hill, he saw a rout of mounted hunters and the hounds coming.

The Ghost saw it as well. He noted what he saw with a ferocious flagging of his ears and a quick lift of his upper lip. But he noted also that the bull's head was turned and held high. The time for which he had waited so patiently had come. There was no gathering of feet beneath him, no collecting of the muscles, however deftly done. From the same position which he had occupied so long and so quietly, he simply shot out through the air, a very low leap, driving all his body so close to the ground that the toes of his hind feet tickled the grass all the way. Fair and true, with the speed of a rock shot from the hand, he whipped under the lifted head of the red bull, and, in passing, he snapped again. The force of his leap and the tear of his teeth jerked him around so that he spun through the air on the other side of his mark and turned a somersault before he hit the ground.

There was only a stifled and choked sound from the bull. The blood was gushing with the beat of the arteries from his throat where the double row of fangs had slashed deep and torn him. He made one last effort to rise and then dropped his nose to the ground and waited for death with eyes fierce and unconquered to the last.

As for The Ghost, he had landed with his head turned away from the bull, and he paid no further heed to his victim. He had performed the task he had set for himself. He had done the impossible. He had actually killed a full-grown bull by a frontal attack. Now he gave his attention to the active group that swept over the hills beyond, while he licked the blood from his lips for a second time.

CHAPTER II

THE CHASE

THEY were close, dangerously close, and The Ghost knew to the last scruple every degree of that danger. Knives and guns and dogs were coming, and, above all, that trebly horrible scent of man which was the one thing in the world he truly feared. Gather under one head all the meaning that was in the scents of the mountain lion, with his claws and his hooked teeth; and the grizzly bear, with downright power of paw and bone-crushing jaws and deep wisdom; and the rattler with glide and strike and poison—add all these items together and put with them a certain mysterious horror, and one may gain some conception of what man meant to The Ghost.

There were a full dozen riders on fine horses; and before them ran a solid pack of wolfhounds, big, savage-jawed creatures who were now running well within their strength, as if they knew that only in a long chase would they have a chance of setting teeth in The Ghost. The vanguard was a round score of greyhounds, running with their snaky heads jerking in and out and the lank bodies flashing in the sun. Half delicate, half clumsily-sprawling creatures they looked as they bounded frantically forward. There had been a time when The Ghost had scorned them, feeling that he could break a dozen of them between his jaws one after another as they came up, but he had learned from experience that a greyhound can

fight desperately long enough to let the main body of
wolfhounds get up.

Something flashed in the distance—sun on a rifle
barrel—and there was a wicked humming overhead
that made The Ghost wince flat to the ground with
down-shrinking of the ears. The sound went through
him like a knife, vibrating electrically. Afterwards
the report of the rifle cracked on his ears like two
sledge hammers swung face to face—a sharp sound
with a ring of metal at the tail of it. This was the
last command. Now he must be off.

The greyhounds were shooting up the last slope
beneath him; it was time, full time for running. He
parted his teeth and gave them a terrible wolf-grin,
and then wheeled and fled over the grass toward the
heart of the hills.

He chose that course because every irregularity of
the ground would be an advantage to him. He knew
that country as a student knows the memorized page
of a book. He knew the short cuts, the ups and
downs, and where one saves strength and time by
going straight up the steepest slope, and where it is
better to take the long way around if one wishes to
conserve the wind.

The greyhounds were perilously close, but The
Ghost began slowly. In his puppy days he had been
apt to break his heart and his wind in the first wild,
hysterical, straightaway sprint. Now he knew that a
fast beginning cramps the muscles and blears the
mind and leaves one broken, whether for fighting or
for more running at the end of five miles.

He went with that baffling wolf-lope which is un-
like any gait in the world. A dog pounds his way
along; a wolf seems to glide along, and, when

watched closely, he seems to be trying to get all four feet ahead of him at once. There is an easy, overlapping play of legs that shoots the body ahead.

Yet he went with amazing speed. To the hunters from behind he seemed merely a gray streak shooting across the green of the grass; from the side he seemed to be galloping lazily, almost. The greyhounds walked up on him hand over hand. He let them come, with one ear flagged back to give word if some unusually fleet rascal had spurted from the pack to nail him. They were almost at his heels when he slipped over the nearest hilltop and entered the broken country. It was toothed with boulders and slashed across with low rock ridges.

The Ghost took the very roughest way because the greyhounds were now so close that he knew they would follow him blindly, for they were running blind-eyed, slavering with the lust to kill, furious with the scent of the game which a greyhound catches only when he is very close up.

Straight through the heart of the roughest of that rough stretch The Ghost led them, and the result was that the sprinting pace broke the hearts of most of them. By the time they reached the far side and the smoother going again, two thirds of the hounds were falling back, or running with labored gaits, their heads jerking up and down, a sure sign that they were nearly spent. They might get their wind and come back for the kill, but at present they were done out.

There remained, however, a thick-grouped set of half a dozen in all, chosen dogs weeded from the rest. The Ghost tried them out by a breathless burst of running for half a mile and then canted his head a little and observed them. The result was that the average speed of the remaining group was sensibly diminished, and, going up the slope beyond, The Ghost increased his gait. Beyond this hill the roughest sort of country began, where the men and the horses would have to make wide detours to follow the chase, and where even the dogs would have a bad time following him. The chase, he felt, was as good as ended as soon as he got across the narrow valley beyond and entered the thick timber.

So he shot over the top of the hill at full speed, breathing deep to make his lungs clean for the last strong spurt of racing—and below him, streaming into the upper end of the valley, he saw five horsemen and a round dozen choice wolfhounds. He was cut off from the rough country and certain safety!

CHAPTER III

MAN-TRICKS

HE slackened his gait. The wind had fallen so that he could hear the gasping of the spent greyhounds far behind him, but the wind held strong enough to bring the telltale scent of man-kept dog, and to bring the crowning horror of the man-scent itself out and up from the valley. As though his eyes alone did not tell him enough!

It was a man-trick—typically a man-trick—and he grinned with rage as he looked down at them. He knew at once what they had done. Guessing that he intended to detour through the heavy going to kill off the greyhounds before he cut in at the rough country where he would be comparatively impossible to follow, the leader of the hunt had detached part of his men and dogs to cut straight across for this valley and block it when the lobo turned.

Now they were waiting there for him, rested, fresh, full of running, and ready to turn him south across the rolling hills where they would have every advantage, and where, by teamwork of the trained packs, they might finally wear him down.

The Ghost shook his loose-wrinkled pelt and snarled as he loped across the brow of the hill. A shout tingled up from the base of the valley; the hounds were cutting straight down the bottom of it to head him off even from the rolling country—to surround him.

His lips wrinkled back from the fangs. He would show them one burst of *real* running. He would teach them some respect for speed!

Down the slope he went like a flash. The fastest greyhound ever whelped could never have measured against that gray streak. A rattling volley, the angry-bee humming overhead, and the kissing of bullets against the grass, showed that the huntsmen were vainly striving to head him off or drop him by a chance distance shot. As well shoot at the wind.

He was down the hill and into the rolling country. The greyhounds were hopelessly out of it now, but they had served their purpose well. They had taken the edge from his appetite for running, and now that he was partly winded, the wolfhounds, running loosely and well, were at his very heels.

Lightning fast, but smooth-gaited as running water, he went up the next slope. It was steep, and there was easier going on either side, but he knew that the main body of the hounds was close enough to follow him more or less blindly. He heard the men whistling as he raced—doubtless that was to encourage the dogs to try for the kill then and there.

The Ghost grinned again. There was reason behind this climb of the hill, for on the other side of it, he well knew, there was a sandy-bottomed gulch thick with shrubbery. They would expect him to go straight across it, or, if he did not appear on the other side, they would guess that he had gone far away down the gulch. But that was not his plan. As soon as he was out of sight in the thicket he would double back at a sharp angle and go down the gulch, doubling on the whole hunt. At the worst the dogs would simply pick up his trail, and there would be nothing lost. At the best, he would gain five minutes, which meant complete safety—or perhaps he would lose the whole hunt on the spot.

So on he went like the wind.

The hounds dropped swiftly behind him, and in a moment more he had dipped over the brow of the hill and shot down into the thicketed gully. It was rank with the smell of sage, and that would probably drown his scent to the hurrying hounds. At least it might delay them.

So he took care to choose his way, never brushing for an instant even the tip of his tail against the foliage for fear that would print his scent for the followers. Straight back down the gulch he rushed, though the loose sand hindered his going. But he rejoiced when he heard the hunt go crashing into the thicket well above him, and then the calling of the dogs faded a little in the opposite direction.

Still he kept up a brisk pace, although the game was, to all intents and purposes, practically done. He had successfully doubled on them, doubled in the very face of men. The savage brain of The Ghost rejoiced.

He remained in the shrubbery for some time, until, sure of his place, he slid out into the basin of that main valley where they had cut him off. The whole pack had gone by. The shrill voices of the greyhounds sounded far off up-wind. The Ghost was once more victorious.

But what was this? What was this deep voice

not so far away, with the deep ring to it, and the
heavy fiber? He whirled into the teeth of the wind,
snarling with incredulous rage. And there they
came! Unbelievably one man had outguessed him
again. There was the rider in the very act of
spurring his horse, in the new direction, while his
"Halloo" sent two rangy hounds away on the trail.

They came like two bullets, great dark fellows,
their long legs driving their bodies forward in
straight lines. They were breathed and rested, too,
by the rest which had been theirs while The Ghost
was laboring through the sand and the shrubbery,
and now they were on his heels as close as ever.

Furiously he took to flight again. There was
no question of trickery or doubling now. He must
show them a clean pair of heels or be run down
and detained until the deadly rifle came up and did
its work. The Ghost ran as he had never run
before. The hallooing of the solitary hunter had
picked up the pack on the other side of the hill.
He heard the noise of the main body far off, rolling
down the wind, but they were nothing—less than
nothing at that distance.

The whole danger had centered now on these two
dogs and on the single horseman. But by evil
chance, the dogs were the best blooded, the best
breathed, the biggest and most formidable of the
whole pack; and the hunter behind them was mounted
on the finest horse of the lot. An incredibly fine
shot, also, for he rode with his rifle in his hand
and pumped in a snap shot time and again, shots
that came perilously close, at times, and always,
in spite of himself, the angry-bee humming made
The Ghost wince toward the ground and falter for

an instant in his running; and each of these faltering brought the hounds yards and yards nearer to
him.

But the battle was by no means over. For the
third consecutive time The Ghost was forced to
sprint, and before ten minutes he was spent. Had
there been only wild blood in him, he would have
wheeled then and fought at bay. But there was
more than wild blood in him. There was that mysterious "gameness" that a dog has, which enables
it to toil on and labor on when strength of body
is gone and only strength of nerve and will power
remains. On this electric reserve The Ghost called,
his tail and his head flagging down a little, and the
breathing coming burningly into his lungs with
great gasps.

The wind was carrying scent and sound of the
dogs to him now, and on the wind, before long,
he heard their gasping as they followed. Plainly
they were not in much better condition. Twice
they spurted, and twice he answered the spurts
and drew away. A third time they put forth their
full strength, and a third time The Ghost answered.
This time one of them came close enough for a
leap, but his teeth closed a fraction of an inch
from the tail of the wolf.

It was a dying effort, The Ghost sensed. The
dogs still labored stanchly behind him, and the
dizzy miles spun underfoot while they followed,
but still they were running with more and more
effort, and The Ghost was beginning to come back
to his wind and to his natural strength, tired by
the frenzy of the long effort, but still with much left.

A few minutes more, and the dogs were growing

exhausted, while he was commencing to recuperate. He could have spurted again; but the wolfhounds were both nearly spent. They were fast dropping back to a dogged gait which they would maintain till they fell. But such bulldogging would never overtake The Ghost, no matter what it might do to other wolves.

He saw another thing now, as he turned his head. The long chase had distanced the man. He bobbed into view only momentarily now and then, on a hilltop, and dipped out of sight into the next gulch. His horse must be spent, likewise. As for the rest of the chase, it was gone beyond sight, almost beyond hearing, laboring vaguely on in the hope that it might come up to view the kill.

But here were two dogs running at his heels; two dogs that would not have dared to chase him a hundred yards had it not been for the support of the master. To be sure they were big fellows. One of them would have matched a common wolf; two would have killed a big lobo with ease. But The Ghost was different, and he knew the difference. A dog fought by training and brain; a wolf fought by instinct; but The Ghost brought all three elements into his fighting.

The mad desire to turn and fight began to make the brain of The Ghost reel. He had been shamed long enough. His decision came over him almost without his own volition. He waited till he had topped the next hill. Looking back, there was no horseman in sight. Then he wheeled and leaped back at the wolfhounds.

CHAPTER IV

UNEXPECTED AID

THEY would fight by the book, he knew. But The Ghost knew the book, also. He leaped as though he were striving to get between them, and, as he had expected, they at once sprang apart so as to take him one from each side and grip at his flanks. But knowing this, they were no sooner separated than The Ghost checked himself mid-plunge, shot sidewise with a sort of sweeping dance step, and rushed the wise-headed dog on the right.

Two dogs on their feet—two dogs like these—he knew he could not match. His plan was shock tactics until one of them sprawled.

His first charge went amiss. The big hound crouched and met the weight compactly, though the impetus of The Ghost crushed flat. But The Ghost, mid-spring, saw that he would have no success here, and changed his mind while he was in the air. He had hardly struck when he wheeled and shot across the back of the first dog at the second.

The latter was taken by surprise, for this first maneuver had taken a fraction of a part of the time that it takes a horse to stamp his foot. He was only half turned as The Ghost's massive shoulder, set for that purpose, struck him and before he could sink in his teeth, the hound was toppled on his back and the under part of him was ripped wide by the teeth of the wolf.

It was like the striking of two blows, and The Ghost leaped and met the spring of the first dog with a clash of teeth. Then he danced away, swift as a phantom. His purpose was a simple one. If he fought and fled at the same time the wounded dog would drop behind—to die later, perhaps. But now he discovered that he could not draw one of the pair away from the other. They had been too well trained to separate, and, moreover, they had already tasted the metal of this foe. Where was the man? And how much time was left?

Far off he saw the horseman coming, spurring desperately; but far away indeed! The two dogs stood side by side, the injured one with lowered head, but still strong as ever, for the loss of blood would not affect it for some moments unless it tried to run.

The Ghost circled them like a playing colt. The sound dog followed him deftly to take the charge, but the injured one was not so agile. The Ghost found an infinitesimal opening and leaped. His teeth gashed the flank; he continued his leap high above the heads of both and landed on the far side. As he twisted to face them the sound dog charged, infuriated by this dodging work. The Ghost met him joyously and gave him his shoulder cunningly low and to the side. He took a rip on the side of his jaw uncomplaining. The dog sprawled. Instantly a foreleg crunched in the teeth of The Ghost, and the wolf shot away to choose his next point of attack.

The dogs were both no better than dead now, and standing back to back, crouching together, one with a foreleg drawn up, and one bleeding terribly from the body, they seemed to know it.

The Ghost tried circling again, and as they swung to meet him, he glimpsed the rider shooting over a nearer ridge of hills. There was short time for work. He determined on a more or less blind risk and charged straight in, his head low as he always kept it for close quarters, for that gave the shaggy hide of his back and shoulders to the teeth of the enemy, and afforded him at least a hope of an opening at the point of points—the under throat.

In this instance, at least, it worked like a charm. One set of teeth closed on one shoulder, and one on the other. Bad cuts, those, perhaps. He cared not. He had twisted his head with snakelike agility, and his great fangs were buried in the throat of the dog with the broken leg. That terrible grip made the other release his own hold instantly. In a moment he was flat on his back. A wolf would have released its grip there and tried to spring away. The Ghost held it until he had worried his forefangs into the life blood. Then he whirled with red-dripping muzzle from that quivering body and snapped at his remaining opponent.

The other had shifted for the throat of The Ghost, but it was a side grip; he had not the wolfish cunning of The Ghost, which taught him the easiest way to get at the seat of life! But at least his grip made The Ghost helpless for biting. He realized it instantly and, at the expense of a badly torn neck, wrenched himself away and flung off at a distance for the last charge. It was only a formality. The final bolt of the dog had been fired; the terrible wound was taking toll now, and his legs were bending under his weight. But before he charged, The Ghost saw the horse on the nearest hill.

He was amazed, first of all, to see that the horse was not in motion, and then he caught the glint of the sun on metal and understood. The rifle was at the shoulder of the marksman. Terror swept over The Ghost, the fear of man. He gave up the second killing, so temptingly near at hand, and wheeled to fly, but as he turned broadside, something stung him through the right thigh and tipped him on to that side as he tried to spring away.

Only that swerving to the side had kept the bullet from plowing through his brain. It seemed strange that so slight a thing should unnerve him, but there was no question about it. Slight though the pain had been, his right hind leg was useless. He found it out as he whirled to his feet, nearly falling again as he made the first stride. Again the gun barked, but this time the bullet sang evilly close, yet harmless.

Behind him the deep music of the hunt was blowing up the wind as he dropped over the hill, running heavily on the three legs—a far, far sound. He would have given it no heed a little time before, but now it meant much indeed. One greyhound, the least of the pack, could finish him now. With bristling hair the great wolf bent to his work, panic-stricken. One dog killed, one dying—surely that was a handsome price for the life of even The Ghost, but the big wolf had no mind for dying. He wanted, at least, some narrow place where he could stand at bay and battle to the death as the king of wolves should do.

It was a marvel that he should run as he was running now, but he knew that it was a short effort that lay within the possibilities of his strength. The blood was flowing steadily from the wounded leg, and now that the numbness was gone he felt a steady ache of pain.

Behind the hill there was the dull echo of a gun; that was when the sick-hearted huntsman killed his hopelessly wounded dog. Back there a voice was shouting; that was the hunter as he called up the rest of the hunt, and his halloo was sending the hounds hot on the blood trail. At that scent of blood a new note came into the voices of the yelling hounds, and the tired wolf heard it and knew its meaning. His own bay had rung with some such note on many a like trail.

Into yonder hills he felt that his strength would carry him, though now the chase was coming perilously near; and in those hills he might find some hole in the ground where he could back. Then let the dogs come at him one by one or two by two, and he would teach them how a death-fight should be made! Or perhaps when he gained some such shelter, a man would come and stand at a distance and kill him with one of those bee-humming bullets. But in that case it was no shame to die. Nothing in the mountains, The Ghost knew, dared face man.

The hunt roared over the hills as he labored up the far slope. He gained the hilltop with the gasping of the hounds close on the wind behind him, and, past the rise, the first thing he saw was the

house of a man, a shack huddled against the side
of the hill. He shrank back, snarling, but then he
saw only the narrow opening of the doorway. There
was a place where he would have shelter for his
back, and there he could turn at bay. In his panic
he bore on again with his broken-gaited lope, and
plunged through the door.

Too late he saw the man inside, close to the
door. He braced his three feet; but the force of
his gallop and his weight carried the bloodstained
monster across the little room and crashing against
the farther wall.

There was a corner. The Ghost shrank into it,
and with his forefeet braced and his red mouth
gaping, while panting racked his sides, he waited
for the finish, unafraid.

The man beside the door had risen, and he was
other than the men whom The Ghost had seen
when he crawled to lonely camp fires in the mountains. He was larger; it seemed that he would
never stop rising as he stood up from the box
on which he had been sitting.

The Ghost saw a marvel. In the hand of the
big man was a glint of metal which was a sure
sign of the wrath of man. That glint of metal
meant bullets so long as he was within range. The
Ghost blinked, and then he saw that, though the
symbol of wrath was in the hands of the man, there
was no anger in his face. The eyes were as calm
as midnight—the still, open midnight of the mountains which The Ghost might never see again!

The hunt crashed and roared over the crest and
would be on them in a matter of seconds, but
The Ghost did not hear it. All he was conscious

of was that large, quiet face, unmoved by wrath, and the steady, watchful eyes. Something swelled in the heart of The Ghost. He did not recognize the emotion. It was a pain that had nothing to do with the body, and with it there was a lifting of the spirit. Strange hopes of he knew not what came to him; a strange security settled over him, though he could see the sharp-headed hounds bursting down the far slope to get at him.

When the hand of the man was raised The Ghost did not wince, for the instinct told him that the blow was not for him. After all, that instinct was not so strange. What was the wild wolf, a million years before, which first felt the power of the eye of a man and, flying from its enemies, crouched at the feet of one of them and whined for help?

Such a sound, at least, formed deep in the body of The Ghost, and it came, swelling his throat to bursting; not the harsh, terrible growl of a wolf, but the whine of a dog!

The big man started with an exclamation, shoved the revolver into his holster, and slammed and barred the door in the face of the onrushing pack. The Ghost heard their bodies crash against the barrier and heard their anxious claws scrape on the wood.

CHAPTER V

THE PARLEY

STERN voices of command hushed, in part, the wild clamoring of the pack; The Ghost heard them scattering, heard them sniffing under the wall of the cabin behind him. He heeded them not at all. There was still power in his jaws to crush more than one throat if the worst came to the worst. It was the men who counted now, and as he heard their voices he crouched still lower, shuddering. One thing he knew distinctly. The door which would have been an impassable barrier to animals was nothing at all to the humans, and the scent of man blew sharp, overpowering, about him. Nothing could keep them away, save the power of their own kind, and that power, it seemed, lay in the huge man who now blocked the open window.

Presently others approached. The Ghost caught outlines of other men beyond the window, and, above all, there was the rider who had followed so long and so closely, the man who had outguessed him, the man whose bullet had plowed the stinging furrow in his flesh, the man whose two dogs he had killed. He was a gaunt fellow, active of foot and hand and eye. That eye now flamed. He had seen the two finest dogs in the mountains, dogs of his own rearing and his own fierce training, killed before his eyes and he wanted a return kill. He went straight to the big man.

"Stranger," he said, "our pack is smelling around this shack on the trail of a wounded wolf. Is they a hole under the cabin he could of got into?"

"I guess not," said the man of the cabin.

Here the other glanced past the man at the window and cried: "Boys, the wolf is inside! Stand away, partner, while I blow his head off!" And he drew his revolver.

But the big man did not stir from the window. "Look here," he said. "Why has the wolf got to die?"

The gaunt man gasped in astonishment; his astonishment turned to anger. "You aim to get the scalp of that beast yourself, eh?"

"I don't want his scalp," said the other mildly. "But I don't want somebody else to get it either."

Fighting rage suffused the face of the hunter. "Say," he began, "if you think you can——"

Here he was interrupted by a companion who caught his arm and dragged him away, while others of the hunters pressed on to resume the strange argument with the man of the cabin.

"Look here, Steve," whispered the pacifier, "keep your tongue under the bit, will you? Know who the big boy is?"

"No, and I don't care," declared Steve.

"You will in a minute. That's Bull Hunter."

"He's big enough to be a bull—but the bigger they are the harder they fall."

"You fool, that's the man who dropped Jack Hood; and that's the man who rode Diablo."

"No!"

"There's the hoss now!"

He pointed to a giant black stallion, close to seven-

teen hands tall, with muscles like a Hercules of
horses and tapered like a sprinter. He was going
uneasily to and fro in a little corral near the house.
A too-inquisitive wolfhound slipped through the fence
to talk to the stallion and was greeted with a snort
and a tigerish rush that sent him scampering to
safety, with his tail between his legs.

"Yes," admitted Steve, convinced and uneasy. "I've
heard about Diablo, and I guess it's him, all right.
But this Bull Hunter—what right has he got to keep
me from that wolf?"

"Listen to him talk and you'll see. Stupid-talking
gent, ain't he? I dunno much about him; just
heard rumors. They say he's pretty soft on Mary
Hood. That's Jack Hood's daughter, the pretty one.
But after he shot her father, of course he had to
run for it. Between you and me they can't keep
a gent as big as Hunter from going back to the
girl he loves one of these days, and when he does
they'll be a pile of trouble. I guess he's postpon-
ing it."

The giant at the window, in the meantime, had
been listening intently to the spokesman of the hunters; and he listened with his brow puckered, and
with blank, dazed eyes, as though it were hard for
him to gather the meaning of the simple words.

"Maybe you dunno what you got in there," he
said to Hunter. "Maybe you dunno what that is.
Ever hear of The Ghost?"

"I'm new to these parts," said Bull Hunter gently.
"But I've heard that The Ghost is a big lobo."

"He is—the worst cattle-killer in the mountains;
the trickiest, biggest wolf that ever trotted out to

raise ruction day or night. That's The Ghost squatting yonder in the corner."

Bull Hunter shook his head slowly. "If he's a wolf, how come he's run into my house?"

It seemed to stump the spokesman for a moment. Then he said: "The Ghost was shot through the leg. The hounds was close up, and he simply was run to death and ducked into your house. But they ain't any doubt 'bout him. Wolf? Why, look! It's written all over him."

Bull Hunter turned and regarded his strange guest with that thoughtful, half-dazed wrinkling of his brows. The Ghost regarded the big man critically. He knew that the voices of the hunters were sharp, aggressive, painful, and threatening to hear; he knew that the voice of Hunter was gentle and pleasant to the ear—a voice that sent a tingle up and down his spine. Now the battery of those two pairs of eyes was turned upon him, and he dropped his head under the shock and watched them with a dangerous lifting of his lip above the fangs, and a roll of his bloodshot eyes. The cuts from the fight with the dogs had covered him with blood, and he made a terrifying figure, big enough for two wolves.

"Look at that!" exclaimed the huntsman. "You say he ain't a wolf?"

He pointed as he spoke, and The Ghost shuddered. He was being cornered. The next time that hand went out it might bear the glint of metal which meant an explosion and then death. The Ghost looked up into the face of Bull Hunter, his sides heaved, and the new sound, the dog-whine, came from his throat. It had a strange effect on the giant. He made a long step toward The Ghost and then changed his mind and wheeled on the man outside the window.

"Ever hear a whine like that out of a wolf?" he asked.

The huntsman himself was barely beginning to recover from his astonishment, but he rallied quickly.

"Wolf or dog," he said, "no man has to look at him twice to see what he is—but, wolf or dog, it don't make no difference. Every man on the range knows him. Every man knows what he's done. He's killed Steve Hendrick's two best dogs, and he slaughtered the big Jordan bull. That's one day's work for him, and it's about enough; but it's only an average day's work, I tell you. Man, the damage he's done runs up into the thousands of dollars every season! Stand aside and let me finish him!"

Bull Hunter stepped aside—and instantly moved back into his former place, blocking the way of the hunter's raised gun. When it was seen that he was determined on resistance, the rest of the hunters drew near with black looks. Into those gloomy faces Bull Hunter stared with eyes which had gradually cleared of doubts.

"Gents," he said, "the way I been raised up is to look on everything that comes into my house and asks for a shelter as a guest, and a guest while he's under my roof can't be hurt by other folks without they put me out of the way first. If a murderer and a thief came to my house and asked me to keep him, I'd do it. The minute he was outside the door again I might try to kill him, but while he was inside I'd treat him like a brother. If I'd do that for a skunk of a man, d'you think

I can turn out a dumb beast that's come and whined at my feet?"

His voice rose a note or two and swelled out largely at them.

"Gents, I can't do it! It ain't in me, somehow. I've got a little money. I'll pay the price of his scalp a good many times over. But while he's inside my house, you keep hands off. I guess that's final!"

He spoke firmly, rather threateningly, and though there were uneasy movements toward guns in the party he faced, there was no outright drawing of a weapon.

Bill Jordan, the oldest man who had ridden in the chase, came out of the rear of the group and, approaching the window, spoke for the first time. He was a withered old rancher with more money than he knew how to spend, and with a reputation for keenness that was widely respected in the mountains. He was rolling a cigarette while he spoke; his whole manner was free from provocation or hint of viciousness; the sting of what he said lay entirely in the words themselves, and not at all in the tone in which they were uttered.

"You're Bull Hunter—Charlie Hunter, I guess?"

"That's my name," said the mild-voiced giant.

"I'm Bill Jordan, tolerable well known in these parts."

"Glad to know you, Mr. Jordan."

"Thanks. I owned that bull that was killed to-day. I've owned a good many other head that The Ghost has butchered—and it's got to be stopped. Is that plain?"

"It sounds reasonable," said Bull almost plaintively. "But you see my position?"

"Certainly," and Jordan nodded. Having finished rolling his smoke, he lighted it, never taking his wrinkled, thoughtful eyes from the face of the big man during this process.

"Now," he went on, taking up a new phase of his idea, "you live up here with a man I've never seen, but I've heard him described as a smallish gent with gray hair and a nervous way with his hands. His name is Pete Reeve."

"Pete Reeve is my partner," said the big man with a sort of childish pride.

"Pete Reeve is a tolerable good sort of man to have for a partner," admitted the rancher, "but if he ain't a man's partner he ain't near so good to have around, I've heard folks say."

"Who?" asked the giant with a ring of danger in his voice. "Who told you that?"

The other deftly turned the subject. "You said you had enough money to pay for The Ghost's scalp several times over?"

"Yep."

"And where'd you get that money? Out of trapping? That's your business, isn't it?"

Another man might have been irritated by this close volley of questions, but the giant remained perfectly calm.

"Yep. I make a good deal of money out of trapping." He seemed to consider the questions of the rancher as implying compliments for his skill. "Maybe you've heard about the pile of skins I bring into town every once in a while?"

His smile of expectancy gradually faded. The wrinkling eyelids of the rancher bunched above eyes that were probing ceaselessly at the mind of the giant.

"And you get all your money that way? Out of the traps?"

"No, some of it is what Pete leaves around. Pete always has plenty of money. Come easy, go easy with Pete." The big man went on artlessly, unaware of the gathering fire in the glance of Bill Jordan. "He always leaves money around, and what's his is mine. So I can pay for the damage The Ghost has done."

"And how does Pete Reeve make his money?" asked Jordan softly.

"I dunno," replied Bull Hunter after a moment of thought. "I never ask much where he gets his money. Pete don't encourage questions none."

Jordan was stroking his chin. He seemed to be changing his mind about Hunter.

"Partner," he said at length, smiling faintly, "you're either the deepest one I ever seen, or else you're a——" He checked himself. Then he went on gravely: "We'll drop this matter about The Ghost for a while. Sooner or later the wolf will sneak out, and then one of us will drop him at sight. But he'll probably slaughter your horse, out yonder, before he's through with you. That isn't my business. It's strictly yours. In the meantime, when Pete Reeve comes back you can tell him that some of us in these parts are a lot more curious about the way he makes his money than you are. We're so curious that we're apt to start inquiring after where he gets it, and when we start inquiring we may come with guns. Don't forget. We've heard stories—no matter about what, and we're interested."

Bull made no reply. He stood expectant, waiting as if for the other to go on.

"You just tell Pete," said Bill Jordan presently, as gravely as before. "Maybe he'll figure out what we mean when we say that the air around here don't agree with some gents, and they find out that they'd be a lot healthier if they moved. You just tell that to Pete and leave the rest of it to him to figure out. Come on, boys!"

He turned to the other members of the chase. They were by no means willing to give up so easily the quarry which they had run to the ground. But the sight of the burly shoulders of Hunter and the words of Jordan at length persuaded them; they finally departed with many a surly look over their shoulders at the little cabin which sheltered The Ghost from their dogs and their guns.

CHAPTER VI

GREAT MOMENTS

WITH troubled eyes Bull Hunter watched them go. When the last of the horsemen had dropped over the ridge, he turned to his strange guest. As for the other problem, Pete Reeve would know how to decipher the puzzle, and Pete Reeve would tell him what they must do.

He found that The Ghost had not moved from his corner. His head was still on his paws, and he crouched in a slowly growing pool. Plainly the animal was bleeding to death.

Bull Hunter ripped a piece of old sheeting into strips for bandages and approached the great king of wolves with his hand outstretched, talking softly. But The Ghost heaved up his head and greeted his host with a terrible snarl. No dog ever whelped could have emitted that throat-tearing sound. It came with a great heave and indrawing of the ribs; the whole power of the big brute seemed to go into that warning. Bull Hunter, instinctively thrilling with horror, nevertheless made another step forward. It brought The Ghost to his feet, the injured right hind leg drawn up clear of the floor, but ample power remaining in the other three limbs. So standing, he lowered his head a little and waited for the charge.

He knew well enough that he had his death wounds unless something were done to them soon, and he knew, also, that to heal those wounds was beyond his power. But between the approach of the soft-voiced giant and the healing of his hurts he made no connection. He had seen men, at a distance, catch horses and dogs, and always they had used these methods of soft-voiced approach with one hand outstretched in sign of amity. Humanity, to The Ghost, meant nothing but a succession of wiles, dangerous stratagems.

The big man had halted at the second snarl, and now he stood looking quietly down into the face of the lobo. The Ghost trembled with fear. It had been thrilling enough, in old days, to crawl to the edge of light circling around a camp fire and wait until the eyes of one of the men went toward him, unseeing, but seeming to see. Then with the shadows to shelter him, he had always felt as if the glance of a man paralyzed his strength.

Worst of all, there was a continual temptation growing in him to give up the battle and surrender to this man as to the inevitable. The Ghost recognized the madness of that impulse with bristling hair and another throat-racking growl. Of course it was the dog instinct in him, and he fought valiantly against it. A strange desire came to him to let that extended hand touch him, and then to close his eyes and wait for what would happen with a vague surety that it would only be pleasant.

He must fight that away. He must find a means of escape. But the door was still closed, and the only way out was through the window. In his one hind leg there was still power, he felt, to carry him through the window with a leap, but the man blocked the way. Therefore the man must be destroyed first. He looked at Bull Hunter, carefully avoiding the face and eyes. He discovered at once that, omitting the face, there was nothing terrible about a human being. Outside of the eyes, there was nothing strange or strong.

The Ghost lowered his head a little more to make ready for the spring, but at that moment the man stepped to one side and raised a broad cloth, such as The Ghost knew men wrap themselves in when they sleep at night. Now the man was out of the path, and however easy it seemed to kill him, The Ghost was wise enough to know that he had better get away without a fight if he could.

At that his move was like the uncoiling of a packed steel spring. Despite the hampering lack of that strong fourth leg, he went at the window with a rush like the flight of an arrow, but just as his nose was in smelling distance, so to speak, of the sunshine beyond the window, a shadow interposed—that cloth in which men sleep was flung before his head. Was it a weapon as well as a shelter, this protective hide which men took off and put on again at will?

He had no time to think twice. The blanket folded about his head, stifling and blinding him, and two mighty arms picked him out of the air and crashed him down to the floor, sending a tooth of agony quivering through every wound in his slashed and battered body.

He bore the pain in silence and commenced to fight. But though the great teeth slashed and tore the blanket, he could not bite his way to the light. He was confused, bewildered, and presently, in the midst of his hysteria, one forepaw was caught and a stout cord passed around it in a slipknot.

To The Ghost his forepaws were what hands are to a man. With them he dug. With them he held down a bone. With them, on occasion, he fought, the stout nails tearing almost like the cutting claws of a cat. With those paws he felt his way over dubious ground. With those paws, tapping with exquisite nicety, he had more than once sprung a trap. The Ghost fought like a demon to get that paw free—to no avail. The rope, serpent-like, twisted suddenly around the other forefoot, and then the sound hind leg was brought up and gathered in the toils of the rope.

The Ghost lay helplessly bound, and knowing his defeat, he recognized it. A true wild wolf would have broken his heart struggling with shame and fear and rage. But the strain of the dog in The Ghost told him that the time for active resistance had passed.

Something touched his wounded leg.

That was to be it, then? And was it not natural that when the man tortured him to death, as he had seen men torture other wolves, his brothers, he should begin by tormenting that already wounded place, sensitive beyond words?

The Ghost locked his teeth and stiffened a little, ready to endure. Vaguely he was grateful for the blanket about his head which kept him in ignorance of the next torturing movement.

He was right. Torture of the most exquisite description ensued. A demon in the torturer instructed him just how to extract the utmost pain. First he thrust through the wound another tooth of prodigious length. Then he filled the wound with a liquid which was cold at first and suddenly turned to concentrated fire. The body of The Ghost quivered, but he lay still and endured. Here the wolf rose in him and taught him the way to die with dignity, yet it was a mighty anguish.

It passed away slowly. Other agonies were being added. Something was being passed around his leg, crushing the wound together, and the pressure did not relax.

But presently the pain diminished. It decreased swiftly. The blood began slowly to circulate where the leg had been numb before. The wound grew warm, and the cunning brain of the wild creature suddenly understood that the process of healing was beginning.

Then a mystery presented itself. What was in the mind of the man? How, by his torture, had he started that process of healing? Not only how, but why? Why did he do it?

The blanket was lifted from his head. It not only let in the fresh air and the light, but it also made him aware of the voice of the man. And then he knew that the voice had been speaking all the time. The terrible pain had made him unaware of it in the conscious mind, but subconsciously the voice had been working on him, building a basis of endurance and assurance in him. Now he was keenly aware of it. He had more strength and calm to be aware of it. For, behold, the anguish of that injured leg was entirely gone!

He rolled a bloodshot eye and looked into the face of the tormentor and healer. That face was not grinning with the pleasure of the torturer.

Now the great hand went out above him—he shrank under it as though the very shadow of the hand were a weight. It descended slowly, slowly, and a wild impulse to swerve his head and a snap came to him. He knew suddenly that no matter how swiftly the man moved his hand, he, The Ghost, could move his head more quickly, and with his teeth he could mangle that hand beyond recognition. But a second thought came. Suppose he snapped once; suppose he mangled one member of the man? The rest of him would still be whole, and he, The Ghost, lay helpless.

He closed his eyes, shuddering, and waited for the hand to touch him.

That hand fell. In the treating of the first wound he had been unaware of the touch of the hand; pain had blurred all smaller sensations. But now, for the first time in his life, he was aware of the touch of the fingers of a man. Oh, strange sensation! A little tingle of electric happiness went down his back, trailing the slow passage of those fingers, and the voice went on at his ear. Strange voice. There was in it the quality of the touch of the finger tips, the same soothing, the same assurance of safety. A cloud of content blurred the mind of The Ghost.

Suddenly his brain cleared. The torment had begun again, and this time with a long, slashing wound on his shoulder. Surely this time he should bite, even in self-protection. The pain grew exquisite. He snapped his head about, and his teeth closed over the hand of the man, and the eyes of the wolf grew terribly green with hate and anger. But the hand was not torn away, slashed by the teeth as it was withdrawn, and there was no break in the smoothness of the voice. In turning his head, The Ghost's eyes had shocked, by surprise, on the quiet eyes of the man.

That shock kept The Ghost from grinding his jaws together and ruining the good right hand of Bull Hunter forever. The man knew that only by a hair's breadth had he escaped catastrophe. His left hand still stroked the back of the wild beast; his right hand still lay on the wound; his eyes still held the eyes of the brute. The neck muscles of The Ghost slowly loosened, his teeth relaxed, his head fell back into its former position, and he waited. Bull Hunter looked at the double row of little white indentations across the back of his hand. From one pinhead puncture a tiny, tiny trickle was oozing. That escape had been close indeed, for if the wolf has tasted—— Even big-hearted Bull Hunter trembled, for he knew that only a man can forgive bloodshed. To the wild ones the sight of it, the taste of it, is the signal for the death-battle.

He went on with his work with a strange peace in his heart, and a sort of childish happiness, for indeed, only a child would have been capable of that pure and calm exaltation of the spirit which came to Bull Hunter in his great moments, and this was one of them. A wild beast had submitted to the power of hand and voice and eye. He felt that he was doing with kindness what all the speed and teeth and guns in the party of the chase had been unable to accomplish.

As to The Ghost, he was infinitely amazed at himself; a little afraid, too, because he had not closed those teeth of his when the occasion presented itself.

CHAPTER VII

A REAL FRIEND

THE treatment of the second wound was the same torture—first a new opening of the wound and then the application of the cold liquid like water which presently turned into intense fire. Twice The Ghost came within an ace of turning his head to bite. Twice he fought back the impulse and waited, for now the pain never grew so great that he was unaware of the voice, and from time to time that slow hand went down his back, and the finger tips left the little electric trails of pleasure behind them. His patience was threefold rewarded, before the end. The pain ceased even more quickly than that of the hind led, and here, as in the leg, there was the flush of comfort, and the pleasant sense of healing begun.

The work went on. For every slash on head and body that process was repeated. When it was over, The Ghost was weak from the many pains; but he was warm with comfort, and still he waited, with his head stretched on the hard floor—waited for what might be coming to him from this man of many mysteries.

Other things happened, now, in swift succession. First, metal clanked, and then a weight of it encircled his neck. The collaring was something new. The smell of the iron, with the man-scent on it, made him tremble a little, but after all it was a small thing compared to much that he had gone through this day of days.

The next marvel was the severing of the rope which bound his feet. The cords had been drawn so tight that the feet were numb for lack of blood, and, while the blood began to circulate again, tingling, The Ghost wondered.

Outside, the wind was rising. It would blow a gale this night, and a chill gale, at that. A dry, sharp, cold wind, The Ghost knew at once—a terrible night for wounds! How could he keep warm if he had to lie here moveless, on the cold wood?

But the work of the man was by no means done. Presently The Ghost heard a sharp rattle of metal. He looked askance. A thing of metal stood in the corner of the room. He eyed the engine quietly, waiting. Perhaps it would waken to life before long. No, it was obviously man-made, rank with the scent of man, as were all things in this cabin; not only the scent of the big man, but of another. The Ghost bared his teeth at the very thought.

The big man was gone through the door, and, left alone in the cabin, The Ghost became uneasy. The scent of the second man was doubly strong now, and from the outside of the cabin came the clear odors where the hounds of the pack had walked and sniffed at the ground. He was more and more troubled. At length he hitched himself into a crouching position, leaning his hindquarters somewhat against the wall of the shack so that the weight was taken completely from his wounded rear leg. This accomplished, he waited for what should happen, more reassured now that he was in a position of some defense. The iron thing around his neck,

he now discovered, was hitched to a place in the
wall with a flexible rope, of iron, also. He tried
it with his teeth at once and discovered that not
only was the taste unpleasant to a degree, but the
hardness of the iron made his jaws ache from the
pressure.

At this point the big man came again through
the door, shut out the wind, and deposited on the
floor some dry wood sweet with the smell of resin.
Then he took paper, crackling more than dry leaves
under the foot of a heavy bull, and put it in the
stove, and presently a match hissed on the trousers
of Hunter, and spurted into flame.

The Ghost winced toward the floor at that sight.
Here was the most dreaded of all things—the play-
mate and helpmate of man. Here was the inanimate
life which he had seen become terrible in the forest,
red and huge and roaring with a voice louder than
the roar of a hundred grizzlies. His pointed ears
worked back and forth, and the hair prickled down
his back as he saw it. Then the paper was lighted
and flamed up.

He backed himself as far as possible against the
wall. He began to understand the meaning of the
chain. Perhaps the man had tied him there, helpless. Now he was setting fire to the shack and
would leave it to burn with The Ghost.

Now wood was piled on the fire; presently the
iron covers were replaced, and a roaring began up
the chimney. That threatening voice filled the wolf
with uneasiness. But the big man seemed full of
cheer. As he walked to and fro through the cabin
he spoke from time to time to The Ghost, and
always his voice was as gentle as ever.

Suddenly the smell of food struck the nostrils of The Ghost, and he grew weak with hunger. Slaver filled his mouth. He gulped it down, and squinted at the face of Bull Hunter. Behold! Red meat, new killed, was under the hands of the man, was being divided, and now a generous portion was placed before The Ghost.

He looked straight over it at the man. Was the big creature a fool to think that he, The Ghost, who a thousand times had sniffed in contempt at man-handled meat with its promises of poison would now accept food which he had seen the hands of a man actually lift and put down?

Bull Hunter shoved the red meat nearer with his foot. The Ghost withdrew from it.

"All right," said Bull, chuckling. "You're a suspicious devil, old boy, but you'll get used to these things after a while."

He sat down on his heels and looked the big wolf in the face. That sudden lowering of his head to the level of The Ghost's own eyes disturbed the latter. It overpowered him with man-presence, and yet the thrill of that nearness was not altogether unpleasant. The man was offering him the meat in his very hand!

A true wolf would never have touched that meat until he was on the verge of starving, and even then he might have chosen to starve rather than to eat. But the dog strain spoke strongly in The Ghost now in one of those rash impulses which overcame him occasionally. That impulse was to play with death, taste death in the very presence of him who might have poisoned the meat.

Cautiously, with his eyes on the face of the big

man, he stretched out his head and with a sudden snap he sheered away a corner of the meat as though with a knife. Then he crouched back with his spoils, snarling terribly. But there was no blow, no anger, no attempt to wrench that stolen meat from his jaws. No, the meat went sweetly down into his stomach in one great gulp. No poison about that mouthful, at least. Perhaps another might be ventured at and stolen in safety.

But would this fool leave his meat still within range? Yes, it was unmoved; it was even shoved closer to him. The wolf looked up in vast wonder and beheld the man laughing! At that a great doubt and a great shame welled up in him.

Never before had he seen a man laugh; never before had he seen that senseless, strange contortion of the face and heard that ringing sound. First he snarled; then he crouched.

Now the laughter rang with redoubled force. At this the trouble waxed great in The Ghost. He wanted to hide his head. He wanted to ask questions. In his big, intelligent eyes a pain of question arose. He stood up on his three legs and suddenly— barked in the face of the man!

It put a sharp period to the laughter. The big man recoiled a step. No wolf since the beginning of time had ever uttered a sound just like this.

"By jingo," he muttered, "you've got a wolf's head and a wolf's body and a wolf's teeth, but you got the heart of a dog and the brain of a dog and the voice of a dog—and—and you are a dog, old fellow!"

CHAPTER VIII

A PARTNER'S CODE

A FLESH wound in a wild animal, so long as the wound is clean, heals with marvelous rapidity; and before many days the wolf was putting his weight on the injured leg once more. There was still a bandage about it; but the other, slighter wounds had been left open for some time; except for the right hind leg, The Ghost was quite recovered.

They had been days strange beyond precedent to him. Every hour his keen nose, his unfailing eyes, his ready ear had been drinking in knowledge. His life had been spent as a wolf; now the dog nature, released, rushed into maturity overnight almost literally. Among other things, the scent of that second man, which had been so fresh in the cabin on his first arrival, was now blurred away to obscurity. It remained keen only around the bunk on the far side of the room, and about certain bits of clothing. The Ghost hated that smell because it was unknown; also, because it was the smell of a man.

His life with Bull Hunter was not teaching him to understand the species. The big man was to him merely the great exception. He had felt the power of Bull Hunter's hand; he had experienced the wisdom and the cleverness of the big man's mind. But this learning had taught him that man was truly formidable, and his close-hand knowledge made him dread all the others. Here was the exception, this man of the calm voice and the wise eye. Here was the man who knew how to turn pain into comfort. But had not the wound been, in the first place, dealt by the hand of a man?

It was for this reason, many nights later, that the big animal wakened halfway between dark and dawn, and crouched lower to the floor.

The night was warm, the door was open, and through it blew the scent of horse and man coming over the hill. The Ghost slid a step toward the bunk of the master, but the master slept. He cautiously tried the strength of his chain. It was as powerful as ever. There was nothing for it but to crouch there and wait and endure.

The waiting did not last long. There were noises —creaking of leather, snort of a horse, behind the shack; and then man and horse odors both approached. The horse odor came from something which the man carried; the man odor was that which had been in the cabin ever since The Ghost came there.

He slid back against the wall so that, in case of need, he could use the full length of his chain for the purpose of a leap.

The stranger came softly, making a faint singing sound beneath his breath. The Ghost had often heard Bull Hunter make a similar sound; but the similarity did not make this the less offensive. Yet he waited without a growl.

Presently a sulphur match spurted into a faint blur of blue light, and then a lantern shone. It discovered a little man with hair streaked with gray and a withering, keen-eyed face. He hung the lantern on a nail, and as he did so, The Ghost made his leap. He had calculated well, aiming to drive his long head just above the man's shoulder and give the full range of his fangs to the soft flesh of the throat.

By one inch he came short of his mark. The chain jerked taut as he shot through the air, his murderous fangs clashed under the chin of the little man. As he fell toward the floor he made a frantic effort to make up for the first failure by settling his teeth in the man's leg. That would bring him toppling down, and, once down, The Ghost would get at his throat.

But the little man had skipped back with a tingling yell, and the Colt winked in his hand with the speed of his draw. The thundering call of Bull Hunter saved the life of The Ghost by the split part of a second.

"But it's a wolf!" shouted the stranger.

"It is—no—a dog, Pete. Let me explain!"

"It's a wolf, and of all the ornery, no-account critters in the world a wolf is the meanest. That one is going to die pronto. D'you think you can turn this shack into a menagerie?"

"Pete, don't you see he's chained? Otherwise you'd be a dead one yourself instead of talking about killing."

The little man rubbed his throat ruefully, still feeling in imagination, the tearing grip of those fangs.

"Besides," Bull went on, getting up from his bunk, "he's not a wolf!"

"Look out!" shouted Pete Reeve, whipping out his gun again.

For his gigantic companion was going toward

him quite regardless of the fact that in so doing he was placing himself in range of the teeth of The Ghost. The Ghost, indeed, had flung himself in the path of the advancing master and tried to drive him back with one of his most terrible growls.

"Watch out, Bull!" cried Pete Reeve again. "The beast is going to give you his teeth. Jump out of line with my gun, and I'll blow his brains out."

"You put up your gun," commanded Bull Hunter, "I'd rather have you shoot one of my legs off than shoot The Ghost."

"The Ghost!" breathed Pete Reeve, changing color. "That murdering devil? Is that The Ghost?"

"That's him," said Bull.

"He's crouching for his jump right now, Bull!"

"I dunno what's got into him," muttered Bull. He leaned over, Pete Reeve quaking when he saw his companion bring his face a foot from the snarling head of the wolf.

"What's wrong, partner?" said Bull to the big animal.

For answer The Ghost whirled, and, facing Pete Reeve, he threw himself back against the legs of Bull Hunter.

Bull Hunter began to laugh. "Don't you see it?" he cried happily. "The Ghost don't know you, and he don't like you. He's trying to keep me from getting near a dangerous gent like you, Pete."

"He don't like me, hey?" grumbled Pete Reeve, gradually adjusting himself to the strange state of affairs which he had found in his shack. "Well, no more do I like him. But—what's it mean, Bull? What you done to him?"

"Treated him like a dog," said Bull quietly, "and

that's just turned him from a wolf into a dog. Look at that. No wolf, no real, full-blooded wolf, could ever be tamed. They're wild all the way through. But this Ghost is half dog, Pete. The wolf shows on the outside; he's all dog on the inside."

"Half dog? Half snake!" said Pete Reeve, partly in disgust and partly with relief.

He sat down on a box and examined the snarling giant more closely.

"My, but he's got a devil's disposition, Bull. And that's The Ghost? But you're right, Bull. I know wolves back and forth and sidewise, and there never was a real one that ever run quite as big or as heavy in the shoulders as that, and there never was one near as broad across the eyes; nor with a coat near as silky as that. Besides, he's clean-skinned. Not the wolf rankness about him."

Bull nodded and looked admiringly at his companion.

"You sure see things, Pete," he said. "I never noticed none of those things."

"I see the outside," said Pete shortly, "but I got an idea you see a lot more on the inside than I'll ever be able to see. But—The Ghost! How come?"

Bull sat down on his bunk. He could not move to another place nearer his friend, for The Ghost squatted before him and checked every attempt of his to advance, with a wicked glint of the eyes and a growl. He looked big as a bear in that lantern light, and thrice as dangerous.

Sitting on the bunk, Bull told the story hastily. While he talked he stroked the great head of The Ghost from time to time, and each time the fingers touched him, the head was lowered a little, and the eyes of the big wolf softened. When the tale was ended, Pete Reeve swore softly with admiration.

"It's you that's got the nerve, Bull," he declared. "The rest of us aren't a thing beside you! Why—maybe you'll get some good out of the brute—and him The Ghost!"

That name seemed to be the big stumblingblock for Pete's astonishment.

"Another thing," went on Bull. "There was a rancher with the hunters. Name was Jordan."

"I know him," said Pete, sharpening with interest. "I know him pretty well. What about him?"

"You say that," said Bull, "as if you didn't like him much."

"I don't. But fire away. What did he have to say?"

"He left a message for you. You see I offered to buy The Ghost for the price of the dogs he'd killed during the chase. Killed two, you see. And Jordan seemed sort of surprised to find out I had that much money."

"And did you pay for the dogs?"

"Nope. They didn't want money. They went off grumbling. They wanted The Ghost's scalp, they said, not the price of it."

"I don't blame 'em. But get back to Jordan. I'll bet he wasn't talking for any good!"

"Well, he seemed to wonder how I happened to of made that much money out of the traps. So I told him that part of the money was yours.. You generally had plenty, and didn't mind if I spent it like it was my own."

"No more do I, lad," said Pete Reeve with a sudden warmth. "But go on."

"He seemed surprised to find out you made so much money. Wanted to know how you made it."

"And you told him it was by prospecting—finding gold claims and selling 'em quick? You told him that?" asked Pete Reeve eagerly.

Bull Hunter flushed and hesitated. "Partner," he said slowly, "I've heard you talk about prospecting and mines. But I've never seen you go out with a hammer and a pick and powder and a drill in your pack. I've never seen you bring home no specimens. I've never seen you with a gent who was going to buy one of your claims. I've never seen you with a single raw nugget. So how could I tell him that you make a living out of mining?"

"Ain't my word good enough for you?" asked Pete coldly, but the frown which he summoned very patently covered a weakness which he felt to be in his position. He did not wait for the answer to this direct question but ran on: "What did you tell him, Bull?"

"I—I told him I didn't know."

Pete Reeve swore. Then he rose and walked quickly back and forth through the cabin with a light, soundless step. Suddenly he whirled on Bull Hunter.

"They's times, Bull, when I think you ain't got any sense!"

The big man nodded. "I'm not very bright," he he said humbly.

At that Pete Reeve's keen eyes softened. "I don't mean it that way. Forgive me, Bull. But why didn't you tell Jordan my story, or make up one of your own just as good?"

"Pete, I ain't got a very good imagination. Besides——" He paused, miserably. "Pete, Jordan is plumb wrought up about you. He told me to tell you a lot of queer things."

"Tell them!"

"Something about a lot of people around here being interested in you and your ways and watching you close. Also, he wanted me to tell you that some folks had found the air around here plumb bad for them and had moved away to other parts."

Pete Reeve came to his feet and stamped. "Did he say that?"

"Don't get riled up. What's he driving at?"

Pete began to walk the floor once more. At length he faced Bull again in his sudden way.

"Bull, what do you think I do when I'm off and away from the cabin for these long spells?"

"I dunno, Pete," said the big man.

"What?"

"I haven't thought," said Bull quietly. "I've worried a pile about those trips of yours, but I haven't dared think."

"Well," cried Pete Reeve, "they were lies that I've told you. Want to know the straight of what I am? Want to know it?"

He thrust the words at Bull with his meager arm extended.

"It's your business," said Bull faintly. "Not mine!" Then he shrugged his shoulders and sat straighter. "But, we being partners, everything that's your business is my business, too. Go ahead and tell me, Pete."

"I can tell you short and sweet. I've lived the way The Ghost there has lived—by taking the things that belong to other men!"

Bull stood up slowly, an enormous, imposing figure in the shadows.

"I've been a man-killer, Bull," continued the shrill-voiced little man in a frenzy of grief and self-accusation such as comes to every one now and then, "just the way The Ghost has been a cattle-killer. And I've robbed and stolen, and fought other men for money I didn't have no right to. That's the truth about me, and if it was ever known they could hang me ten times for what I've done. There's the truth. And now get out and leave me. Go your way, and I'll go mine!"

He had expected an outburst of emotion; the calm of the big man stunned him.

"Why, Pete, if it's that way, it looks to me like you had more need of me than ever."

Pete Reeve gasped and choked. "You mean that, Bull?" he whispered. "You mean that?"

"You and me being partners," said Bull slowly, "of course I mean it."

CHAPTER IX

JORDAN'S SCHEME

BILL JORDAN was an impatient man by nature and by training. He had warned the entire countryside to be on the watch for Pete Reeve, and he had arranged to call up a posse at a moment's notice. But after he had alarmed the entire widespread community, word came that Pete Reeve was no longer going on the strange journeys, but had settled down to the peaceful life of a trapper, in company with big Charlie Hunter. Men began to say that Bill Jordan had gone off half-cocked on this topic of Pete Reeve's lawlessness.

But Bill Jordan was certain he was right. He decided that either his warning had frightened Reeve into a temporary quiet, or else the little man had made so much money in his recent raids that he had determined to settle down, for the time being at least. All of Bill's preparedness went for nothing.

This was intensely irritating. It put him in the position of a false prophet, a rôle for which he had no liking. He determined finally that if Pete Reeve would not fall into the way of temptation he, Bill Jordan, would send the temptation to wait on Pete Reeve. After all, it was a simple plan, worked on the theory that animals which cannot be shot in broad daylight may often be trapped by night. Bill Jordan had arranged for the trap, and now he set about finding bait for it.

Here accident played into his hand, for, on a trip to Willowville, interesting tidings were told him by the sheriff. No less a person than Bud Fuller, suspected of many crimes and distinctly not wanted in most parts of the mountains, had felt the urge toward a peaceful life and had approached the sheriff, offering to give bond for peaceful and law-abiding conduct if the sheriff, on the other hand, would guarantee his support. For Bud Fuller had defied the law and law-abiding citizens so long that he now needed protection. This the sheriff hesitated to extend to him.

To Bill Jordan the news was manna from heaven. It gave him new life, and he instantly unfolded his plan to the sheriff. The sheriff listened first with wonder and then with a grin of interest, for the plan of Bill Jordan was that Bud Fuller should show his intention of becoming a peaceful citizen by first acting as a decoy to take in another one of the lawless. In a word, Bud Fuller should be the bait for the trap which was to close over the head of Pete Reeve. The sheriff doubted the possibility of using Bud for a bait.

"He's a fox, and Bud Fuller is a fox," said the sheriff, "and it'll take a cleverer man than either of us, Bill, to use them together."

"Poison fights poison," insisted Bill Jordan. "You send for Bud Fuller and just leave the rest to me."

Accordingly, Bud Fuller was sent for. He was a middle-aged fellow with a worn and solemn face; his smile was a painful thing to see, and it twisted ironically to the side of his face. That smile appeared when Bill Jordan, in the presence of the sheriff, made his offer. The smile even persisted

when the sheriff in his turn, as soon as Jordan
was silent, announced that if the scheme were put
through he would see that people were kept from
troubling Bud Fuller, and he could manage this by
the simple and efficient expedient of making Bud a
deputy sheriff.

"Listen, gents," said Bud Fuller when both had
finished their speeches, "do either of you know Pete
Reeve—well?"

"I know he has a long record; just what that
record is I can't say," said the sheriff.

"Nor nobody else can say," declared Fuller. "No-
body else knows just what Pete Reeve has done.
Speaking personal, I don't want to know.   But
I've run into enough stuff about him to know that
he's one of the hardest gunmen that ever packed a
Colt."   He turned on the sheriff.   "You remember
Denman?"

"Sure."

"Was he bad?"

"One of the worst."

"And a fighter?"

"Fight a bull with his bare hands."

"D'you know who finished him?"

"No."

"Pete Reeve.   And they's others.   I could go on
talking, but I won't.   No, sir; give me an easy
job while you're at it.   No Pete Reeve in my game."

Bill Jordan had been thinking hard and fast.
Now he entered the argument decisively.

"Look here, Fuller, you want to go straight.   But
there are a pile of gents who won't believe that
you've quit your old game, and there are a pile more
who don't care whether you've quit or not.   They're

on your trail, and they want to get you. Is that straight?"

At the latter part of his speech Fuller winced and then thrust out his lower jaw, but it was the savagery of desperation rather than of courage.

"I know! They want me bad, some of the boys!"

"And who's going to keep them away?"

"The—the sheriff. It's his job."

"You know the sheriff can't be your bodyguard. It's public opinion that's got to protect you, Bud. You ought to see that. Just now public opinion ain't for you. People around here don't think much of you, if you want me to be frank. They think you're just down here as part of another of your games. What you've got to do is to prove that you're on the side of law and order. Once that's proved, everybody will be your friend. You can count on the gun of every law-abiding citizen, and they're the people who will make these parts too hot for any one that's after you. Bud, ain't that something worth having?"

He concluded swiftly: "Maybe you will run some risk with Pete Reeve. But you can take care of yourself with him or any other man, and——"

Here Bud broke in: "Don't make no mistake there. Sure I can take care of myself with most any man. But Pete Reeve is different. I wouldn't have no chance agin' him, and I know it."

"But think it over, Bud. How will he ever suspect you?"

"He's a fox, I tell you; a wise old fox, and he'd smell me out!"

"Then make your choice, Bud. Either you follow my plan and help us catch Pete Reeve or else you stay here—unguarded, helpless; and the first pair of your enemies who happen to get together, there'll be an end of Bud Fuller. But it's nothing to us. Make your choice!"

It was a brutal way of putting the situation; but Bud Fuller was sufficiently brutal himself to be appealed to by such methods. For a long time he sat with his head bowed and his forehead corrugated in thought. When he raised his head his eye was dull and his face resigned.

"I'm going to take the chance and make the play for you," said Bud Fuller, "but the chances is ten to one that this job will finish me."

The sheriff and Bill Jordan apparently appreciated the importance of the decision. They rose in turn solemnly and shook hands with him. Then Jordan entered into the final detail of the scheme.

When it was finished, Bud made no delay. His horse stood saddled before the building. Five minutes later he was jogging out of town.

He headed straight for the little shack where Pete and Hunter lived, and camping that night on the way, he jogged into the vicinity of the shack a little past noon of the next day. It was a commonplace, sun-blistered little building, but the heart of Bud Fuller leaped in him as he saw it, for there was to be performed the first part of the most exciting, important, and dangerous adventure he had ever undertaken in a life crammed with action and fighting.

Bud let his pony jog on slowly, and dismounting before the door, he set about beating the dust out of his trousers with his quirt; through the door he looked straight at the profile of little Pete Reeve.

Something about the expression of the formidable

gunfighter, and something about the tenseness of his position, made Bud Fuller stop beating his trousers with the quirt and stare.

Reeve sat tilting forward on a box, his face set, his right hand twitching toward his hip. By something about his eyes, Fuller knew that some object was approaching steadily, an object which Pete Reeve viewed with terror.

Fuller was bewildered.

Then a deep voice boomed from the shack: "Steady, boy," and into the range of Bud's vision came the ominous head of an enormous wolf, carried close to the floor, the gray, terrible head of the lobo.

Instinctively Fuller brought out his gun, wondering why Reeve had not shot already. Then he noted that the lobo carried a red cloth in his mouth.

"Down! Down with it!" said the heavy voice from the hidden part of the shack.

The huge head slowly sank still lower. At the feet of Pete Reeve the red handkerchief was deposited, and then the giant wolf, whose powerful shoulders also had come into view, winced away with a snarl of hate.

"That's enough!" cried Pete Reeve. "If I have to face that four-footed devil coming toward me again I'll lose my nerve and go for my gun. No more, Bull."

"The minute you go for your gun he'll go for your throat," the deep, smooth voice said, and chuckled.

"But," cried Reeve, "it's facing death, I tell you, Bull!"

"Not a bit. I can stop him in the middle of the air with a call. Try it, Pete."

"Not for a thousand dollars! If you're crazy,
I'm not!"

Here Fuller, wondering, approached the door and
showed himself. He saw, at the far end of the
shack, the great body of the wolf backed up between
the knees of Hunter and snarling at the man before
whose feet he had just deposited the handkerchief.
No wonder the nerve of Pete was nearly gone. It
was the face of a wise devil in the skin of a wolf.

"This beats me!" cried Fuller. "A tame lobo!"

"Tame devil, you mean," said Reeve, rising and
mopping his brow. "And I'd trust him just as far!"

He turned to Fuller and extended his hand with a
rather drawn smile.

"How are you, Fuller? What are you doing in
these parts?"

"Just happened along; nothing special in mind,"
said Fuller.

"Glad to see you. This is my pal, Charlie
Hunter."

"I've heard a pile about you, Hunter," said the
newcomer, approaching with a cheerily extended
hand.

He was stopped by a terrific snarl from the wolf,
that made him jerk his hand back to his revolver.

"Devil is right!" gasped out Fuller, eying the
bristling wolf dog in horror.

"Just a minute," the big man said, grinning, "and
I'll send him out. Go talk to Diablo, boy. Look
yonder!"

He went to the window and pointed out. The
Ghost followed, and, having cast a snarling look
over his shoulder to make sure that the other two
men were at a safe distance behind him, he reared,

and planting his forelegs on the window sill he looked out. Raised in this fashion, he was well nigh as tall as a man. The big hand of Hunter stroked the head of The Ghost while he talked.

"Go out to Diablo. He's waiting for you; getting so he misses you, partner!"

The Ghost turned his head, flashed a glance up into the face of his master, and then made for the door. He went slinking close to the wall, giving the two men ample chance to look at his huge white fangs as he went. At the door he was transformed into a gray streak that whipped out of sight.

"Now look here," called Pete. "This is worth watching!"

He led the way to the window, and, looking out, Fuller saw the great lobo clear the fence of the corral with a mighty bound and land in the middle of the inclosure. Instinctively Fuller cried out in horror, for in that corral, also, stood a black stallion, a mighty animal fully seventeen hands tall, it seemed to Fuller, and exquisitely limbed for speed and endurance in running. He thought to see the next leap of the lobo carry him at the throat of the stallion, and again he reached for his gun; but the giant beside him laid on his arm a grip that paralyzed the muscles.

"Easy," he said. "They're friends!"

And indeed the wolf dog, instead of springing again, turned slowly toward the stallion, who approached with pricking ears and lowered head. Before the startled eyes of Fuller the two big, beautiful animals, each a king of his kind, touched noses; and then The Ghost stretched himself at ease in the shade of Diablo.

CHAPTER X

SETTING THE TRAP

"AM I seeing things?" breathed Fuller, watching with fascinated eyes. "How come?"

"His work," said little Pete Reeve, nodding to Bull Hunter, not without pride. "Nobody but Bull Hunter could of done that with a wolf. Though why he spent the time on him I can't say."

"Wolf?" echoed Bull Hunter with a sudden anger which surprised Fuller, who had heard much about the equable temper of the big man. "Wolf? Who says he's a wolf? Look at that head! Is that a wolf's head—really? Is that fur a wolf's fur? And ain't he got all of a dog's ways? I tell you, he's a real dog; just cast in the shape of a wolf, that's all!"

Pete Reeve winked at the newcomer as much as to say that this was a sore topic with his companion.

"It took Bull a whole month of steady work—five or six hours a day—to teach The Ghost that he wasn't to jump at Diablo every time he seen him."

"The Ghost?" cried Fuller. "Is that The Ghost?"

"Right!"

Reeve enjoyed the thrill of this announcement.

"That's him. The rascal snooped up to my fire one night. But how come he ain't been shot by one of the ranchers around these parts? Last I heard they all hated him like poison, and then some."

"They've tried to get him," Reeve said, nodding, "but Bull here went down to the village and paid every claim he could find agin' The Ghost, and after that he promised to break the heads of the first crew that tried to pot The Ghost near the cabin. The Montgomery boys didn't think he meant it, and they come prowling up here. Luckily they missed The Ghost the first shot, and before they could get a second bead on him, Bull was at 'em."

Reeve laughed at the exciting memory.

"They was a ten-second argument. After that Bull picked up one of 'em under each arm and brought 'em in here, and we patched 'em up and sent 'em home ag'in."

"And the Montgomery boys is big men," said Fuller thoughtfully, eying the giant with new interest.

"They are," said Pete quietly.

To escape from this embarrassing talk Bull found some excuse which brought him outside the cabin.

"Don't like to be talked about," said Pete, chuckling. "Bashful as a girl, the big fellow is. He's all gold, Fuller."

Then his face straightened as he met the eye of Fuller quizzically turned upon him.

"Now, Bud, what's up? I know you ain't just happened by here. You never just happen by any place. What's the game?"

Fuller was delighted to have the subject broached so frankly.

"The biggest, easiest game you ever was led to," he said ingratiatingly. Then he saw that Reeve was nodding with understanding rather than enthusiasm.

"I knew it was something like that. Ain't you heard the news, Bud?"

"What news?"

"I've gone straight."

"No!" cried Bud, admirably affecting surprise.

"It's true. But Bull is enough to turn any man straight. Funny thing if he couldn't do it. Gent that can make a wolf into a law-abiding dog ought to be able to teach a growed-up man some sense."

"You didn't act like you was particular fond of that law-abiding dog," said Bud, artfully refraining from making a direct attack on the little man's conscience.

"Didn't I? You mean when he was bringing me that handkerchief? Well, I admit I ain't. But it's Bull's idea that The Ghost has got to learn to know me, and I've got to go through an hour of torment every day. Yesterday Bull made me pat his head!"

Pete wiped his brow, which glistened with perspiration at the memory.

"Had to pat the head of that man-killing devil, with him crouching and snarling and begging Bull to give him a chance to go at my throat! Well, this day's work with The Ghost is over. Hadn't been for you coming, Bull would of kept me at it another half hour!" He smiled gratefully at Fuller. "To go back to your proposition, Bud, I ain't interested. Mighty good of you to come to me, but Sandy Lawson is in these parts, and Sandy could act side kicker to you as well as any man."

"Him? Sandy Lawson? I'm man enough to do anything Sandy can do. I don't take many partners, and when I do I want a man!"

Reeve would have been more than human had he not melted a little before this compliment. He smiled and shook his head.

"You see," explained Bud, "it's got to do with cracking a safe. I'm not a bit of good with the soup—and you're a wonder at that game. I need you bad, Pete."

Pete grew more sober than ever.

"What's in the back of your head, Bud?" he asked sharply, at length. "You know me, and I know you. But we've never pulled a job together before. Why bother me? I take it for a compliment, but why not go back to one of your old partners?"

The making or the breaking of his game was before Bud, and he rose to the occasion with a master stroke. He got up from the chair and turned coldly on Pete.

"If I ain't good enough for you," he said sternly, "I guess that's about all the talking we need do. I can get along without you, I guess."

"Wait a minute," said Reeve. "Don't get hot in a minute. I'm off any safe-busting, or any other business. But I don't want you to go away misunderstanding me."

"I ain't misunderstanding you, I hope," said Bud. "But listen to me, Pete. Gorgie is dead; he was my old pal. And Lammer is in the jug. So I'm left alone. That's why I've come to you."

"I knew Gorgie was dead," admitted Pete thoughtfully. "But I hadn't heard about Lammer. Too bad, Bud. Why don't you take that as a signal and break away from the game?"

"I'm going to after this deal," said Bud. "But this one was too big for me to pass up."

"How big?"

"Only eighty thousand dollars," said Bud, drawling the words.

Pete gasped.

"Eighty thousand dollars," went on Bud, avoiding

the face of Pete and musing, as though already planning how he would spend his share of the money, "and it's in a tin box you could split with a can opener. Easy! Eighty thousand for picking it up."

"And how far?"

"Get there before midnight if you start at dark, or a little before."

Pete sighed and shook his head. The temptation was vast. He had not saved up a great deal of money, in his life of adventure.

"You ain't talking to me, Bud," he decided. "Sorry, but you ain't talking to me. Drop it!"

Again Bud showed his intelligence by failing to press his request.

"Matter of fact," he said a little later, "I think I can manage the job all by myself. It's a rickety old safe. And I have all the time I want. Blockhead hired me to guard his safe! He's away from his ranch, and they ain't nobody but me there. Can you beat that?"

"I can't raise that," said Pete dryly. "He hires you to guard his coin, and then you grab it from him? No, I sure can't lay one over that!"

"Don't get me wrong," protested Bud. "This gent is about the orneriest that you ever seen. Don't see nothing but the worst side of everybody. Don't really trust me, but he figures they's no way into the safe except through the combination."

Bud chuckled at the idea.

"What's his name?" asked Pete.

"You ain't been long in these parts," said Bud cautiously. "Probably you wouldn't know him."

"Try me."

"Bill Jordan is his name."

Bud knew that there had been one clash between Jordan and Reeve already. He had saved this shot for the final effect, and he was not disappointed. Pete Reeve came out of his chair as though an invisible hand had jerked him up.

"Jordan?" he said through his teeth. "That skunk?"

"You know him?"

"Know him! It was him that threatened to run me out of the country!"

Pete Reeve bit his lip nervously, drew out his revolver and looked to its action, shoved it hastily back into the holster, and then looked with a strange mixture of dismay and eagerness at Bud.

"I'd give ten thousand if I hadn't seen you to-day, Bud," he said.

"Why?" said Bud innocently.

The reply was an oath. Pete Reeve hurriedly left the shack, but Bud smiled his lopsided smile and nodded in content. He knew that he had hooked his fish, and now that the hook was in, it might be well to let the fish run for a while instead of attempting to land him at once.

Patience was rewarded. Within ten minutes Pete Reeve had come back into the shack.

"Are you sure about the coin?" he said abruptly.

"Dead sure."

"Then I'm with you."

"Shake!"

"It's for to-night?"

"To-night."

"And then I'm through."

"Me, too," said Bud, with more meaning than Pete Reeve could guess.

CHAPTER XI

THE RESCUE

IT was not difficult to make their excuses to Bull Hunter. Bud told the big man during the afternoon that he preferred, as a rule, to make his journeys by night during the hot weather. As for the absence of Pete Reeve, he was merely riding a step or two along the way with his old friend, for Bud was leaving that region, and would not be back for many a moon.

The grave face of Bull Hunter did not change by one iota during this explanation. He heard it from Bud, in fact, with his head turned partly away, stroking the big head of the lobo; but just as he himself was nodding to the explanation, The Ghost lurched a little forward.

Bull became thoughtful. It was the invariable habit of the big animal to twitch forward in this uneasy fashion when some one winked at him. A dozen times he had done it when his master had blinked inadvertently. But who could have winked now? Bud Fuller, of course, winking at Pete Reeve, as much as to say: "You and I know the real truth about this night's journey."

And Bull, still with head bowed, lest they should see his emotion in his raised face, knew sadly what was coming. The long inactivity of Pete had at last proved too much for him, and now he was about to start on another wild career. Yet Bull was wise enough to make no protest, give no advice, offer no plea. Pete had practically promised to give up the old life, and when a man breaks a promise it is foolish to remind him of it. Friendships that have lasted half a lifetime are destroyed by just such strokes. So Bull said nothing but waited gloomily for the dark and their departure.

They left, however, while the twilight was still bright, waving carelessly to Bull. He watched them drop over the hill, and absently he stroked the head of The Ghost, who had whined with pleasure the minute the two men disappeared. The Ghost's conception of happiness lay, apparently, in the absence of all men other than the master.

So on this evening The Ghost whined with pleasure when he saw that they were to be left alone. He picked the red rag of a handkerchief off the floor—that hateful rag which he had so often been forced to carry to little Pete Reeve—and took it into hiding in a far corner. Some day he promised himself the pleasure of tearing that rag into small bits.

But as he dropped it in hiding, the master appeared behind him, stooped, and picked up the rag. After this he began walking up and down the shack, and The Ghost followed at his side, whipping back and forth close to the wall, and always keeping the face of the master in view. The big man was in thought; his decision was a sudden leaving of the shack, bearing the saddle over his arm.

The wolf dog followed, rejoicing. The saddle meant a long ride on Diablo, and those rides were always a joy to The Ghost. They gave him a vague taste of his old life. The moment Bull swung into the saddle and sped across the hills, The Ghost started at his gliding gallop, with which not even the gait of Diablo could compare. That frictionless lope kept him up with the stallion and carried him easily far ahead. He had learned from the frequent calls of his master during other rides that he was never to pass out of sight or out of hearing. That apparently was against the law. So he merely wove a loosely twisting trail back and forth about the straight line of the stallion's course; and as The Ghost ran he was reading the story of the night, his accurate dog-nose noting every sign.

Presently, on the horizon straight before them, he saw two riders against the sky; and shooting to the left, his nose caught the scent of the little man's horse. They were following Pete Reeve, then, and his companion! If that were the case he would overtake them at once. He loosed himself into a few seconds of wild running, only to be caught by the soft, controlled alarm whistle of the master. He turned and found that Bull Hunter was sending his horse cautiously down the slope, taking advantage of a clump of trees which he artfully kept between him and the two distant riders of the night.

The Ghost paused with his head on one side, to think. The manners of a stalking man are the manners of a stalking beast, and it was apparent to The Ghost at once that Bull Hunter was chasing the two rather than trying to catch up with them. It ceased to be a stupid ride. It gained an interest, even an excitement.

Now The Ghost glided off into the night, and on the top of the next ridge, he flattened upon the ground. Sure enough, the two horsemen were in the midst of the next gully, traveling leisurely. The

Ghost looked back and saw the master coming swiftly.

"Good boy!" said Bull kindly, when he came up. "Find 'em again."

The Ghost darted ahead in obedience to the forward wave of the arm. Obviously the thing for him to do was to act as a halfway point, keeping sight of the two horsemen himself and remaining in view of the master, who was thus in touch with the two at second hand, so to speak. Had not The Ghost seen the coyotes hunt in packs in this manner, one clever scout bringing on the rest of the pack?

He loved the game and played it perfectly, and while he easily kept the horsemen from catching a glimpse of him, it was easy also for Bull Hunter to keep in view the gray body of the wolf, like a ghost indeed through the starlight and in the clear mountain air.

At length The Ghost halted and waited for the master again, and Bull came up in time to see the two indistinct figures pause before a house and then dismount.

Every doubt left him when he saw that the windows in the big house were blank, unlighted. They had come to rob. Bull slid from the saddle and leaned against Diablo in an agony of suspense. But what could he do? He would never be forgiven if he interrupted his partner at work, and yet in some manner he must intervene.

A low growl from The Ghost made him aware that the wolf dog was running back and forth, heading slowly up wind, his nose held high to catch some blowing scent; and the sound of the growl distinctly meant "man."

Bull peered in that direction, and finally he saw, drawing swiftly out of the night, a group of a round dozen riders. He called The Ghost back with a soft whistle, and with the wolf dog beside him, an interested onlooker, he watched the proceeding of the newcomers. Strange proceedings, indeed, for they left their horses with one man, near a group of cottonwoods, and began to spread on foot in a loose circle around the house. More than a dozen. There were fifteen or twenty of these silent hunters, and there could be only one thing they hunted—Pete Reeve!

How could he reach him? To try to charge through the line was the worst sort of folly. He might indeed break through, but that would only mean that he would be cooped up with his partner. He could act better as a rear guard, and strike at the critical moment by surprise.

Below the hill he could see the cordon spread. Odd that they should have arrived so pat after the two disappeared inside the house. Was it not possible that this Fuller had played the part of traitor? He had hated the man's twisted smile; instantly he was sure. But while his blood grew hot, he was still thinking. There must be a warning given to Pete. Perhaps by discharging his revolver? No, that was a clumsy method.

Then the idea came to him. He took out an envelope, and, with a stub of a pencil, he wrote blindly in the dark a few words. This he wrapped in the red handkerchief of Pete Reeve and placed it in the mouth of The Ghost. The big animal snarled with anger, but Bull hushed him.

"Quick!" he said, and, as The Ghost started off

toward the house, Bull struck him on the flank sharply.

It turned The Ghost into a running streak, but in spite of his speed, he was using cunning, also. He had seen the glint of metal in the hands of that spreading cordon, and he was of no mind to come in sight of one of those stealthy hunters. Bull, grinning with pleasure, watched The Ghost fade into a gully and disappear. The gray streak appeared again directly before the house and was blotted out in the dark of the interior.

It was not difficult for The Ghost to find Pete Reeve. The scent was as plain to him as pointing arrows to a man. It led through the open door and up the stairs, then down the upper hall; The Ghost twisted into a dark room on the third floor.

A single lantern light showed Bud Fuller at the window and Pete working busily before the safe. It was the exclamation of Fuller that called Reeve's attention to the big wolf dog. He turned as The Ghost crouched, for Bud Fuller had made that inevitable movement toward his gun which, to The Ghost, meant battle instantly. But the movement was not completed, and The Ghost rose from the floor and slipped to Reeve. At his feet he deposited the red handkerchief.

"Well," muttered Pete, "the fool dog has got in the habit of chasing me with that red rag."

He picked it up gingerly from under the snarling nose of The Ghost, who began to back slowly toward the door. No sooner had Pete's hand touched the handkerchief than he felt the stiff paper beneath. He took it out, and at once the sprawling, heavy, almost illegible handwriting of Bull stared him in the face.

"House surrounded. Fuller crooked. Break for high hill in front of house. I'm there."

That was all. Pete, crunching the paper slowly in his hand, turned on his companion. He said nothing. He was too dazed to show even a great wonder, but Bud Fuller knew instantly that his hand had been shown in some mysterious way, and he went for his gun like a flash. In the stupefaction of the moment the hand of Pete Reeve was chained. That would have been his last battle had there not been help from another quarter, and that help came.

The telltale move of Fuller's hand had caught the eye of the wolf from the door, and instantly he leaped. Already the gun was clear of the holster when he shot into range of Bud's vision, and with a startled cry the latter turned and threw up his shoulder to save his throat from the fangs. His throat was saved, but the fangs of The Ghost crushed in his shoulder, and the next instant the weight of the big animal, lurching around, whirled Bud and flung him against the wall. His head struck the sill of the window, and he slipped, an inert pile, to the floor.

The Ghost released his grip and leaped back into the middle of the room, ready for a second attack.

But Pete Reeve was already at the door. To kill Bud meant a pistol shot, and a shot would be warning to the men outside. Silence was his most valuable ally now.

As he ran down the stairs The Ghost rushed by him, with paws that scratched on the floor below, and then disappeared outside the house.

Pete followed more slowly, and venturing cautiously out onto the veranda, he scanned the ground about the house. The cordon of the watchers had taken shelter here and there behind small mounds of earth, and not one was in view, not even a glint of metal from their guns. There was nothing for it save to spring from the veranda onto the saddle and send home his spurs in vague hope that he might take them by surprise before they could enter an effectual fire upon him. As he slipped toward his mount a faint voice cried from the upper part of the house: "Help! Help!"

It was Bud, regaining his senses, and his shout was what saved Pete Reeve, for it started the cordon on a run for the house, expecting to find their quarry already engaged in battle with Bud. To their amazement a figure leaped from the veranda onto a horse.

There were three men of the cordon directly before the house. Before they could halt in the middle of their run and turn their guns on the fugitive he was through their lines, riding low over the pommel of his saddle. They sent a scattered volley, which failed to bring him down, and then dropped to their knees for steady rifle work.

As they did so, a gun spoke from the hill before the house, and bullets crashed into the wall behind them. They took to shelter before they tried another shot; and by the time they were in shelter they could hear the beat of Reeve's galloping horse, but the man himself was a shadow bobbing against the sky line over the hill.

Bull Hunter was swinging into place on Diablo as his comrade shot past him; but twenty of the black stallion's long strides carried him to the side of Pete. He saw Reeve's head turned toward him; but not a word was spoken, and as soon as they were beyond the next ridge of hills they turned north, away from the shack where they had lived so many months.

They could never go back to it again, and they swung north at a steady gallop; the sound of the pursuit crashed away in the opposite direction.

The moon came up late that nightt. It found the two horsemen toiling up the slope of the higher mountains, the same mountains toward which the wolf had directed his run when the hounds chased him. When the moon was bright, Pete Reeve stopped his horse, and Bull followed that example.

The Ghost sat down before them, looking steadily up into the face of his master.

It was characteristic of Pete Reeve that he neither complained to Bull for following him, nor directly thanked him for that rescue, but he said with a sort of wonder: "What beats me, Bull, is that you save the life of a wolf because you love the critter; and then he turns right around and saves the life of a gent that he hates. Can you beat that?"

"No," said Bull, "I can't beat that."

CHAPTER XII

BEFORE THE CAMP FIRE

THE camp fire had changed from bright to dull gold, and finally, being chiefly a wisp of smoke and a bed of dying embers, it threw only enough light to pick out the forms near it, in flat, black shadows. The faces of the two men were indistinguishable, but their silhouettes were strongly contrasted. One was a wide-shouldered monster and the other was as remarkably meager as his companion was large. He sat with slumping shoulders like an adolescent child.

"Look at 'em," said the little man. "Look at The Ghost working at the cur, Bull."

The big man leaned and stirred the embers. "I been watching, Pete, all day, and I been wishing that Dunkin would come back and look after his dog."

"Take care of him?" asked Pete. "Why, it looks to me like the dog could take care of himself. The Ghost is fair busting himself to make friends."

"I dunno," sighed Bull. "I dunno." And he shook his big head.

In the meantime they continued to observe the two dogs. The Ghost was peaceably stretched beside the camp fire, doing his best to make friendly advances to a mongrel cur that lay within the circle of the fire's warmth.

It was an important time in the life of the huge wolflike dog. This was his first definite avowal of his change of caste. He was attempting to make friends with the big, fierce mongrel on the ground by the fire.

His methods were not altogether competent to inspire friendly confidence. They began when, after a long survey of the mongrel, he rose from his place beside Bull Hunter and began to stalk around the other dog in a wide circle, moving with stiff-jointed steps that showed he would be instantly ready to fight if the occasion demanded.

The mongrel flattened his head to the earth and watched the progress of the gray giant with rolling eyes. He bared his teeth, but he had not the courage to growl. A growl would be a challenge, but the bared teeth merely showed that, while he invited no trouble, he would fight to the last ditch, if the pinch came. In the meantime he gathered his hind feet well under him, every muscle of his legs quivering and ready to send him off in a flying leap should The Ghost stop his promenade and attack.

The Ghost made no offer to fight. He continued to move solemnly about the other, viewing him from every angle. Finally he went straight up to the other, and standing not a yard away, pricked his ears and slowly wagged his tail. The mongrel twitched his own tail, but it was a perfunctory response.

To make his meaning clear, The Ghost turned and marched about the camp fire in a swift circle. Plainly he was inviting the other to come with him for a romp across the hills, for he looked back as he ran. The mongrel shuddered and pressed his body closer to the warmed earth. Follow that slayer into the darkness, he seemed to ask.

The Ghost returned and now stood with his head

cocked to one side, regarding the other with a wistful curiosity. There was a certain pathos in his attitude, as though he were striving mightily to learn the language of this fellow and finding it impossible. At last his impatience found vent in a deep-throated growl. His antics had been all dog, but his growl was all wolf.

"I think maybe you're right," said Pete Reeve to his companion, hearing the snarl of The Ghost. "In five minutes they'll either be friends or fighting. Dunkin may come back and find himself minus a dog." He chuckled again. "And that'd sure make him mad. He loves that dog."

"He won't be minus a dog," answered Bull Hunter.

"How come?" asked the little man. "You don't think the cur, yonder, would have a fighting chance against The Ghost?"

"The Ghost would kill him in five seconds," said Bull soberly, "but I promised Dunkin when he left that I would keep The Ghost away from his dog. So I must."

"I remember," said Pete Reeve. "When Dunkin left he swore you'd have to account to him if anything went wrong with his dog." He broke off and laughed softly. "Dunkin is a pretty hard sort, but if he knew you better he'd have sooner bitten his tongue than talked so big to you, Bull."

Bull Hunter waved this implied compliment away. "Where has Dunkin gone?" he asked.

The little man jerked his head to one side and looked intently at his companion. "Ain't you guessed?" he asked sharply.

Bull Hunter shook his head.

"Well," said Reeve in the same sullen manner, "I

ain't handing out any information. Besides, I don't altogether know. I ain't riding with Dunkin to-night."

"I think I guess," said Bull Hunter sadly.

The big man's mind was full of doubts. Dunkin, who had joined them a few days before and had ridden off that morning, was an old acquaintance of Pete's; and Dunkin was on the face of him a "bad one." Bull had from the first moment hated the swagger of the fellow and his thin-lipped, twisting smile and his malicious eye. He had not the slightest doubt that Dunkin had left their temporary camp to ride off on some errand of mischief. And Bull, writhing at the thought, felt that his crime would be the greater of the two, if he accepted the hospitality of the other. But what should he do? Could he leave Pete Reeve a hopeless victim to the evil influence of the depraved Dunkin?

It seemed that Reeve's mind had been running in the same direction, for now he said: "Men are like dogs, Bull. I'm like The Ghost, except that he's big for his kind, and I'm little for mine. The Ghost has run wild all his life and raised the devil. So have I. The Ghost found a friend in you, and now he's trying to turn decent and be civilized. I found a friend in you, too, Bull, and I'm doing the same thing as The Ghost. I'm trying to get civilized and live decent. But I don't think The Ghost will stay tame; he'll turn wild again, and so will I."

He sighed and shook his head. "And in the end we'll both have to leave you, Bull."

"In the end," said Bull, smiling sadly, "I'll have to follow you." He turned his head sharply. "Steady!"

The Ghost obeyed the command by springing six

feet backward. He stood with head lowered, a snaky, formidable, cunning head, seen thus in profile. The mongrel twitched himself about and faced the gray giant in the new position.

"You see," said Pete Reeve, "that The Ghost can't make friends with the cur, and so he wants to fight him; if you won't let him fight, you and him will have trouble. And then he'll leave. A wild dog ain't never going to be really happy with a tame master. A man with the wolf strain is just the same way."

In one respect, at least, he had spoken the truth. His voice was hardly quiet when The Ghost, having tried in vain all manner of friendly advances toward the dog, and having been repelled with terror and disgust at each attempt, gathered himself and flung straight at the mongrel. The latter stood up with a brief howl of terror, wavered for the split part of a second between a desire to run and a knowledge that he would be overtaken instantly if he fled, and then bared his teeth to meet that attack as well as he might.

But The Ghost was not one of those who strive to win battles by sheer bulk and brawn, regardless of the punishment they receive. He was one of those terrible and wary fighters who slash another to pieces without receiving much punishment in return. Now, though he came like a driving arrow at the mongrel, he intended no battering assault. He swerved and, shooting past the other, slashed him down the shoulder as he shot by; then he whirled at a little distance for another charge.

The mongrel was himself an old and practiced fighter. Against an ordinary wolf he would have put up a fair battle, but he was unable to cope with this whirlwind of muscle and teeth. He turned to meet the new attack, but he turned too late and would have received the great teeth of The Ghost in his throat, had not a rescuer intervened. Bull Hunter lunged up and across the fire, a mighty figure. His two outstretched hands caught the breast and throat of The Ghost, as the wolf dog sprang. Despite his weight the shock staggered him. For a moment they stood, a strange pair of combatants, the wolf dog forced erect on his hind legs and almost as huge as the man.

The battle lust was hot in The Ghost. He had forgotten that it was his master who checked him. He only knew that this was a bar which kept him from getting at the mongrel again. All his primitive killing instincts were aroused. Twice, swinging his head from side to side, his teeth clashed as loudly as the closing of a steel trap, as he strove to get at the arms of the man. Before he could bite again he was lifted high up and cast crashing down to the ground.

The force of the fall stunned him. When he gained his feet he stood trembling on his braced legs and growling feebly at his master. Then, his brain partially clearing, he backed slowly away, slinking closer and closer to the ground.

Bull Hunter followed him carefully, his hand extended, his voice softened almost to pleading. "Steady, boy. Couldn't let you kill. Steady, old boy!"

"He's gone, Bull," said Pete Reeve, with a sort of cruel satisfaction. "There's all our work undone by one taste of flesh." Then he broke into shrill, mirthless laughter; for it had been a horrible thing to see, that battle of the man and the wolf, and, having been greatly moved, Pete laughed, for it was his nature to go by opposites.

But laughter was the one thing which the wolf dog dreaded the most. This was the one attribute which no animal other than man had. This was the thing which The Ghost trembled at and shrank from, and he had loved Bull Hunter because the big man rarely laughed. There was no mockery in his nature.

Now the laughter of Pete Reeve came to The Ghost as the final blow. He had been beaten and crushed by the physical strength of a man; and now the sense of man's superiority was borne to him in derisive mockery. He turned upon Pete Reeve with a snarl so terrible that the little man instinctively reached for his gun; then The Ghost wheeled and faded instantly into the friendly night.

That was his country; fire light was the country of man.

CHAPTER XIII

THE LOCKET

FILLED with dread, Bull Hunter first followed at a quick walk, then broke into a run, shouting after the fugitive. But presently he saw a faintly outlined form glimmer on the top of a hill and dip away on the other side, and he knew that The Ghost, whose confidence he had won with such pain and trouble, whom he had come to love as if he were a human friend, was indeed gone and had fled back to his own kind.

Bull came back to the camp fire, stumbling like a stunned man. Pete Reeve, in the darkness, failed to note the emotion of his friend. He broke into fresh laughter.

"He ran like a whipped cur, Bull. He's gone back to his cattle killing. I think it was more my laughing than your throwing him down that drove him off."

His fresh peals of mirth fell away to silence when the deep, stern voice of Bull Hunter cut in on him. "Yep, it was your laughing that done it. Otherwise I'd of won him back. It was your laughing and your friend's cur dog."

The face of Pete Reeve wrinkled with pain and flushed with anger, but he controlled himself instantly. If he were a little inclined to mock the big, slow-moving, slow-thinking fellow in ordinary times, on occasions when Bull Hunter became grave, Pete

Reeve instantly showed his respect. He held out his hand now.

"I'm sorry, Bull," he said. "Come to think of it, that was a fool thing I done, laughing at The Ghost when he was kind of on edge that way."

Bull Hunter accepted both the hand and the apology. It was impossible for him to hold malice for more than a moment. But when he sat down again by the fire, he was buried in deep and gloomy thought.

The neigh of a horse far off, a tired horse returning to its home, broke in on his reflections; presently he could make out a horseman climbing the hillside below them. Pete Reeve was already on his feet, gathering wood to freshen the fire.

"It's Dunkin," he said, "and he's come back lucky, if he's come back this early."

Presently Dunkin came out of the night and dismounted into the lights of the new-leaping flames of the camp fire, a lithe, long fellow with a sinister face. He was gayly clad for a desert rider, with all the cow-puncher's finery of spurs and boots and silk shirt and neckerchief and big bandanna, Mexican style. But the dust of long riding had reduced his flaring colors to a common drab. He greeted his companions with no word, but drew a small sack from one of his saddlebags and flung it with a melodious clinking down on the ground by the fire.

"There it is," he said.

Bull Hunter dropped his head, but Pete Reeve picked up the sack and weighed it with a brightening face. "All good stuff, Dunkin, eh?"

"Good stuff? Would I take it if it wasn't?"

Pete untied the mouth of the sack and peered inside. "I wished I'd been along with you, Dunkin."

"I'd rather have you along on a party than any gent that ever wore spurs," said Dunkin flatteringly, "but you wouldn't be no help down yonder in that country." He waved toward the lowlands. "If talk gets dull for me when I'm down yonder, I just mention your name, Pete, and then they buzz around like a lot of hornets. Old Culver come in and raised the price on you by fifteen hundred, and that's started a new posse on your trail."

"Know which way?"

"Just exactly the wrong way," said Dunkin. "They sure don't dream you're up here."

While Pete cooked for the newcomer, the latter sat down on his heels to smoke a cigarette and tell of the adventure.

"It was easy. I just sort of happened to be walking down the road when old man Hood drove along in his buckboard. He stopped to chin, just the way I knew he would. First thing off he seen the saddle marks on my trousers. But I started telling him a cock-and-bull story about losing my hoss, and pretty soon I got up close and shoved my gat under his nose. He's a fast one on the draw, but he didn't have no chance that way. I had him cold. Well, I went through him and got his guns, and the old cuss had two of 'em. Then I grabbed the bag. Pay roll for this month, I figure, and a stake that'll float us for a pretty long time.

"When he seen me with the bag in my hand he loosened up and began to get fresh. So for that I went through him again and got his own wallet with fifty in it and a locket that was strung around his neck. He went plumb nutty when I got that and told me I'd burn in hell for taking his daughter's picture off'n him. But who's been cutting up my dog?"

The last was a veritable yell of astonishment and rage, as the mongrel, with his wounded shoulder, crawled to the feet of his master. Luckily for him The Ghost had slipped a little in his spring, and his snap, as he shot past, had been a fraction of an inch short of his intention. Therefore the wound was a shallow gash which would heal quickly, but, in the meantime, the crimson scab made it seem like a death wound.

"The Ghost," said Pete Reeve.

"That murdering wolf of yours!" exclaimed Dunkin, trembling with anger, and he stalked over toward the big man.

Size meant nothing in a gun fight, and Dunkin was a fighter with guns and guns only. The bulk of Bull Hunter made him only an easier target. So Dunkin was fearless. He hated the quiet honesty of the big man; he hated him because it was Bull who kept Pete Reeve from running amuck on the long trail. Now all his hatred came trembling in his voice.

"You can say good-by to that dirty wolf," he declared, "and you can say it pronto. Where is he?"

"Cleaned out," said Pete Reeve, watching the two in growing anxiety, for he saw Bull Hunter raise his head for the first time, and though he made no reply to Dunkin, Hunter watched the face of the man with a strange steadiness that foreboded no good. "He cleaned out, Dunkin, and it was Bull that saved the hide of your dog. He took The Ghost by the throat and banged him on the ground."

It may have been the words of Pete; it may have

been that the quiet, straight-looking eyes of Hunter cooled the ire of Dunkin, for his tone changed at once. "Took The Ghost by the throat with his bare hands—that dirty wolf?" asked Dunkin. He retreated a step, watching Bull Hunter with a new respect.

"That was what he done," said Pete dryly. "Here's your chuck ready; come on and eat. Besides, on account of your dog, Bull lost The Ghost, and he was sure fond of him."

"That's a pile different," admitted Dunkin. "Makes me kind of sorry I busted out like I just done." He fumbled in his pocket and then he drew out a chain and locket. "Here's that picture I pinched. Maybe you'd like to see it. Ain't it a hummer?"

Bull extended his hand and took the trinket. Awkwardly he snapped the locked open. It was a beautiful subject, beautifully done. A miniaturist of no mean ability, wandering through the West to regain his health, had painted it, and he had done justice to his sitter. With an exclamation of delight Bull Hunter received the trinket reverently in both his opened hands.

"Hit the flint that time and drew a spark, I reckon," said Dunkin, stepping back. "Bull's all wrought up, Pete."

The little man rose and went to his big friend and looked over the shoulder of Bull at the painting. It was a beautiful, dark-eyed girl, and the play of the firelight gave a peculiar illusion of life to her smile.

"It's her," said Bull Hunter at last. "It's Mary Hood, Pete."

He closed the locket suddenly and stared at Dunkin as though he were angry that the eyes of the man had rested on even the representation of that face. "You took it off'n her father, you say?" he asked coldly.

"Sure, son."

"You robbed him of it, maybe?" went on Bull.

Dunkin saw the new drift at once and met it willingly. "If you don't like it because it was grabbed, give it back to me at once."

"It's got to go back to her," said Bull gravely, "and your hands will never touch it again."

Dunkin choked and then cursed explosively. "Go back to her? Not in a million years. Give that to me, Hunter. You hear me talk?"

Pete Reeve drew away and watched quietly. He seemed to be judging the two men.

"Not in a million years I won't give it back to you," said Bull, rising to his feet. "They ain't a man here that's good enough to carry her picture around. This is more'n most pictures. It's so like her it's almost as if there was part of her in it. Not one of us here is good enough to carry this around. It's going back. Mind that, Dunkin."

"Now, by——" began Dunkin.

But Pete Reeve intervened decisively, walking between the two men as if they had not been on the verge of gun play. "You listen to me, Dunkin." And he took the arm of Dunkin and turned him away.

"I'll finish talking to you later," said Dunkin, looking at Hunter and going off with the little man.

"Now," said Pete Reeve softly, when they were well out of earshot. The dwindling camp fire had grown starlike behind them, even at that short distance. "I'll tell you that you was close to a bad bust, partner."

"Because of him?" asked Dunkin. "Say, Pete, them big ones are too slow, a lot too slow."

"I've seen him fight," said Pete with conviction, "and he can shoot. I taught him how."

Dunkin had been prepared for protest, but the last words made him close his mouth with a slight intake of breath that was almost a gasp. The speed and accuracy of Pete Reeve with a gun were grimly known facts in the mountain desert.

"There ain't any fear in him," said Pete. "He's gentle as a kid. But don't make no mistake. He's the worst man to tangle with that you ever seen."

"I ain't taking nothing from nobody," said Dunkin with a sort of defensive ferocity.

"You don't have to. He won't ever mention it again if you don't bring it up, and he won't bother you none."

"I don't think he will," said Dunkin. "Look back there! If he ain't rolling up in his blankets!"

"That's his way," replied Pete Reeve. "When most of us want to do a thing we start right off, but Bull Hunter sleeps on it first, and then he starts to do it. But the point is that it always gets done. In the morning he'll start, and he'll get there. He loves that girl, Dunkin. He seen her and loved her, but he got in a fight with her father—the same gent you stuck up to-day. You know Jack Hood is fast with a gun, but he was like a gent in a dream compared with Bull. Bull shot him down and hurt him pretty bad. Then he got away from the whole Dunbar outfit, including big Hal Dunbar himself, with me helping a little."

"Oh," said Dunkin, "you were there." He spoke as if the whole mystery were explained by Reeve's presence.

"Of course," went on Pete, "after shooting the girl's father he couldn't very well stay around and make love to the girl, could he? Besides, he doesn't think he's good enough to have her wipe her shoes on him. So he's stayed away and ate his heart out, not even talking about her to me. Now here's the point of all this. Bull won't leave me, and he won't let me leave him, because he's afraid I'll start wrong ag'in. And me going near crazy for lack of something to do. Well, in the morning he'll try to get me to ride with him to the Dunbar ranch to see Mary Hood. But you and me will slip away before morning, and I'll leave him a note, saying we got a plan to work out, while he's riding up to the Dunbar ranch. Is that clear?"

"Clearest thing I ever heard," rejoined Dunkin joyously. "Pete, you and me working together can make a million. I always thought so!"

CHAPTER XIV

BULL RIDES DIABLO

THUS it happened that Bull Hunter, waking and standing up from his blankets in the first light of the morning, found not a sign of Reeve or Dunkin or the dog. Only the great black stallion, Diablo, lifted his head from the place where he was cropping the dried grasses and whinnied a ringing good morning to his master. Aside from Diablo there was no living creature. The Ghost was gone, Dunkin was gone, and his best friend, his tried companion, Pete Reeve, had vanished like the wind. There was only Diablo and the mountains in the lonely morning light.

He found a note pinned to the bottom of his blankets:

DEAR BULL: Me and Dunkin have a little trip ahead. I know you ain't very happy about that sort of a trip, and I figured if you knew we was leaving, you'd come along just to take care of me, even if you had business of your own on hand. But I know that you're all set on going to the Dunbar ranch to see Mary Hood. And I sure don't blame you. Go and see her, and look sharp. Because Hal Dunbar and Jack Hood would both give a year of life to get a shot at you. I'll come back and find you later on. Good luck.

But, no matter how the letter was phrased, Bull felt that it was a case of desertion, plain and simple. Two great blows had fallen, one after the other. The Ghost was gone, and now Pete Reeve had followed, all in the space of a single night.

As if Diablo knew the heavy heart of the master, he came in a swinging gallop up the hill, circled the dead ashes of the camp fire thrice and then plunged to a halt before Bull Hunter, a magnificent creature, close to seventeen hands. If Diablo were a mustang, then certainly he was a freakish throwback to the Barb type from which the horses of the Western plains and mountains developed. But no Barb had ever stood such a type. Perhaps a strain of thoroughbred had crossed on the mustang blood. But whatever the reason, Diablo was a glorious picture of a horse.

Now, with his bright eyes gleaming and his forelock blowing in the wind, he seemed to invite the master to gallop with him over the hills. The heart of Bull Hunter lightened a little. He passed a gentle hand over the proud curve of that neck and murmured a word or two in that kind voice which horses love to hear.

He dared not stay long in the camp, for fear that he would begin to brood over the memory of the two whom he had lost. First he cooked a quick breakfast and noted with a pang that Pete Reeve had purposely left behind the choicest and best of their provisions. He found, too, tucked into his saddlebag, a fat money belt with a comfortable supply of coin. It warmed his heart. It also made him wince with the realization that all these days he had really been so dependent upon the little gun fighter.

Breakfast over, he made his pack, strapped it behind the saddle and was off across the hills on Diablo. Two shadows rose repeatedly, a gray wolf running before him and coming back to leap up at the nose of Diablo in playful ferocity, and a little withered man with wise eyes, who had once ridden beside him. But Bull Hunter drove the memories away by main force and allowed himself to see only one thing, the noble head and the shining neck of Diablo; and he allowed himself to dream but one dream, that he was to see Mary Hood!

How he should again gain that great objective was beyond him. She was the daughter of the foreman of the greatest ranch in the mountains, the ranch owned by Hal Dunbar. The foreman he had shot down; Hal Dunbar he had foiled in a first effort to obtain Diablo. Besides, Hal Dunbar was expected to marry Mary Hood. Indeed, all things conspired to make the wished-for interview difficult. Dunbar, Hood, or any of their men, he well knew, would shoot him on sight without question and make their explanation later. But Bull Hunter let ways and means take care of themselves. His first task was to get to the Dunbar ranch.

It lay south, far south, over difficult ridges, a country steadily rougher and more beautiful. Three days went into that long ride. Some of the fat came off the sides of the stallion, so that, when the saddle was taken from him at night, Bull Hunter could see every muscle of the shoulder and hip, could have picked them out with thumb and forefinger, almost. But he was not worried. He merely knew that Diablo was being trained down to racing condition.

In the rose of the dawn of the third morning he crossed the last range and came in sight of the big domain of the Dunbars. It was indeed a kingdom by itself, fenced with mountains in all directions and lying on a pleasantly rolling plateau.

There was fine tillable soil in that sweep of country. A little was already under the plow; a thousand times as much could be put to close cultivation, when a cleverer owner took the reins. Yet in a way it was better that there should be no such thrifty control. It left the fields wide and open, with only random fences; thousands and thousands of acres, spotted with single trees and lofty groves, and cut with pleasant watercourses and tumbled in places with long lines of natural hedges.

Bull Hunter, sitting his horse, atop the crest of the range, could see it all. He could see the great grove of trees near the center of the domain, marking the house of the owner. He could even make out myriad small dots in the nearer pastures. Those were the grazing cattle. The wind changed and blew the musical sound of their distant lowing to his ears.

Such was the kingdom of the Dunbars. Bull Hunter was filled with a kind of sad happiness, knowing that Mary Hood was one day to be queen of it. If there was a sadness about his worship for her, it was only that she was removed to a great distance from him. She was to him like a masterpiece to a connoisseur, a dream of reality rather than an image of what had once been real.

It was dangerous work, for Bull Hunter of all
men, to approach the ranch building in broad daylight, but he was not thinking of danger. He
was feeling his nearness to the girl, and worst of
all, he was coming up toward the rear of the house,
in which direction the barns and stables and corrals
stretched.

On this side also was the long bunk house, sure
to be filled with men who had not yet ridden out
to work, and all of the Dunbar men were sure to
be hard riders and good marksmen. They were led
by the redoubtable Jack Hood and by the yet more
celebrated Hal Dunbar.

Bull Hunter rode in a dream. He came out of
the dream and the forest at the same time, and he
saw before him first the corrals, then the ranging
stables and the bunk house, and beyond, set off
with great terraced lawns and gardens, the house of
Dunbar itself. The sight shocked him. He felt
for the first time keenly the temerity of any single
man daring to brave all this power. A moment later
his abstract alarm was given a point.

A rider swung out from behind the nearest shed,
saw the big stranger, shouted once in shrill alarm
and then whipped his horse about and spurred out of
sight, still shouting and crouched over the saddle-
horn, as though he feared a bullet might follow
him. His fear was so real that Bull Hunter instinctively reached to the butt of his Colt.

CHAPTER XV

THE CHASE

IN a moment his smile went out. The fellow had ridden in fear of his life, and now that Bull Hunter reflected, he remembered him to be Riley, the right-hand lieutenant of Hal Dunbar, particularly in all acts of deviltry.

Riley had fled in fear of death. If the men of Dunbar expected Hunter to shoot to kill they certainly would act likewise. The first impulse of Bull was to gather up his reins, turn Diablo, and send the black stallion across the hills at full speed. Certainly he had been a fool to blunder upon the house in this manner and call out the whole Dunbar force in pursuit.

Yet he hesitated. He was cold with fear, and yet there was an admixture of pleasure in his fear. There is something besides terror in the heart of the wolf as he flees from the pack of hounds. There is a fierce joy in the hunt, even though he is on the dangerous end of the work. For one thing, the imp of the perverse tempts the fugitive to dally with danger. Again there are chances to turn swiftly and rend the leading pursuers.

Some of these emotions made Bull Hunter remain quietly on the black stallion, wasting invaluable moments. Diablo himself seemed to understand that he should be off. He was dancing with short steps and tossing his head and snorting softly, as though he would reprove his careless master.

And now shouts echoed and reëchoed through the chill, quiet air of the morning. The alarm poured through the barns. It reached the house. Bull saw half a dozen men run out from the building and, standing on the terraces, peer down at him. It would have been the simplest thing in the world to pick him off with a rifle at that distance.

That knowledge at last wakened him, and yet he stayed a single instant longer. Where the great doors at the entrance were swung back, against the darkness of the interior, stood a girl dressed in white. Mary Hood, perhaps? At least his heart leaped as though he had been close enough to distinguish the features of her face. He caught off his hat and waved it with a shout, then turned Diablo and sent him away at full gallop, as a rout of the hunters poured out at him, a dozen men riding close together, between two of the outlying sheds.

They wasted no time. The thing to do was either to drop Bull Hunter with a chance shot early in the game, or else to accept a long and exhausting chase, for the running powers of Diablo were well known. Therefore the moment they came in view they scattered, pitched their rifles to their shoulders, halted their horses and opened a close fire, but they found no easy target.

Diablo was running as Bull Hunter had taught him to run for the sport of it, taking the hardest course among the trees and dodging back and forth like a jack rabbit, in spite of his burden and his own great size. At that shuttlelike motion of the target the bullets flew wide. More than one of them sung perilously close to Hunter, but presently he reached denser forest, and the trees were a shield behind him.

At once he called Diablo back to an easy pace. He did not wish to wind the stallion in the first stages of the journey; moreover, the pursuers were not apt to try to outsprint the great black horse. They were more likely to trust to wearing him down on account of the weight of his rider.

In the meantime the hunt grew in number of voices behind him, and he could hear parties cutting to right and left, spreading out like a fan, so that he would have no chance to escape by doubling back, once the chase was fairly under way. By the uproar he guessed rightly that every man on the ranch had taken horse to join in the kill. That would be an easy way to win praise from Jack Hood, the sour old foreman, and money from Hal Dunbar. After the fall of Bull Hunter, Hal Dunbar would ride Diablo.

That thought made Hunter frown. He quickened the pace of the black, and so broke out of the forest which surrounded the ranch buildings, and came to the wide-rolling meadow lands. What he had suspected was true. The whole body of hunters was not sprinting their horses after him, but one section of four hard riders. Far to his left they were driving their mounts with quirt and spur, and the obvious plan was to send out one group after another, while the main body followed at a moderate pace behind and could come up to overtake the fugitive, when Diablo was worn down. It was, after all, the oldest form of "jockeying."

One word to Diablo, and he was stretched to full speed. And what speed it was! It had been many a week since Bull loosed the big stallion, and as the rush of wind cut into his face he marveled. Not Bull alone, but the whole body of the pursuers gave a shout of wonder, as they crashed out of the forest and saw Diablo sweeping away. He ran as though a lightweight jockey were on his back, and the leading group of riders shook their heads. But there was nothing for it but to ride their horses out.

There was Hal Dunbar shouting the order as he came out of the forest. He rode a big gray, strong enough to carry his weight, but, because of his strength, nearer to a draft horse than a runner, for Hal Dunbar, handsome of face and huge of limb, was as big as Bull Hunter himself, and only one horse in the mountain desert could have carried such bulk with speed, and that horse was the black stallion which now carried Hunter away to safety. Hal Dunbar, spurring in vain to keep up the pace, cursed his horse and Bull Hunter and his men and himself. At that moment he would have paid with the value of half his ranch for the possession of Diablo.

That change of ownership, whether to be accomplished by a bullet or money, was at least postponed. Diablo stepped away from the chase as though the others were standing till. Bull Hunter, glorying in the speed, let him run at his will for half a mile. Then he began to think and called him back to a smooth canter. Even that pace was safely holding the fastest of Dunbar's men, and Dunbar himself was out of sight in the rear.

What ran in the mind of Bull Hunter was that, if every man on the Dunbar place had taken horse

to follow him, the ranch house itself was left un-
protected. It only remained to cut in behind them,
and he could get back and see Mary Hood without
danger of interruption—a thought that proved that,
if Bull was stupid as a strategist, he had some tactical
good sense.

But it was not altogether an easy thing to double
back. The chase had spread out widely. Far to
right and left he saw one little group after another
topping the hills and dipping out of view into the
hollows, until it seemed that a small army was following him.

They rode at a steady, hot pace that would enable
them to take instant advantage of any mistake on
the part of the fugitive. Not until they struck
the mountains, certainly, would he have a chance to
double back, and even in the mountains it would be
nearly impossible.

Twice the ranchmen sprinted from the flanks in
an attempt to come up in point-blank range before
he could get Diablo away; twice he forestalled them.
But how keenly he missed The Ghost now! The
Ghost, who would have loafed behind and, ranging
across the front of the line of the pursuers at a
speed that made a mock of horseflesh, would have
come to him like an arrow to report every fresh
threat of danger! But there was no wolf dog.
Neither was there a Pete Reeve who would have
turned in the saddle and kept the pursuers far back
with snap rifle shots. Two thirds of his strength
was gone with them; what remained to him was
not a large ability to plot, and the only trick he
could think of was a childish one in its simplicity.
It consisted in increasing the pace of the black

as they approached the foothills, cutting over to one side, as though he wished to reach a certain pass well ahead of the right flank of the cow-punchers; and then, having drawn them in that direction, trying to cut back across their whole front, as soon as he was behind the first screen of hills. It meant calling on Diablo for two bursts of speed, one as he went to the right, and a far greater one as he dashed to the left among the hills, across the whole front of the enemy, but Bull Hunter trusted implicitly to the stallion.

Two miles from the hills he altered his direction sharply to the right and let Diablo out, so that it seemed he was running hard to make the pass. The moment he did it the whole posse drew together and spurred hard, particularly on the right, to gain the pass before him. They might as well have tried to outfoot the wind. Diablo at three-quarters speed gained hand over hand; before the pass was reached the squad to the right drew up their horses and began to pump volley after volley toward the pass, in the hope of turning the fugitive.

Bull Hunter, by a very simple expedient, let them think that they had succeeded. He allowed himself to lurch far to the left in the saddle, like a man struck by a bullet, straightened slowly, and then turned his right arm dangling loosely, and shook his left fist at the posse. After that he turned Diablo toward the hills before him.

A prolonged yell of triumph came ringing and tingling through the air after him. They had winged their quarry, they felt, and the wounded Bull Hunter would do the natural thing and try to put as much country as possible between himself and his pursuers, so that he could dismount and tend to his wound. In this case he would drive the stallion straight across the range.

So they bunched in and followed in that imaginary line, while Hunter, as a matter of fact, as soon as he was behind the first screen of hills, veered the black sharply to the left and, bending far forward in the saddle, let Diablo run as he had never run before. The voice of the hunt rolled to him over the hills, nearer and nearer. He must not be seen and he must not be heard. He might, for all he knew, be in front of the very middle of the hunt. But he took the chance, and reaching a dense grove of young lodgepole pine, he wedged his way into them and waited.

In less than thirty seconds the first of the hunt appeared well behind him. They made no delay. In the tangle of hills before them, a dozen Diablos, with a dozen giant Bull Hunters, might be riding. Straightforward they spurred their mounts. Another group and another followed, drawing in toward the center, spurring hard. Their voices crashed against the opposite slopes, and in another moment were lost in the confusion of hills.

The last group and the closest drove past the clump of lodgepoles, not fifty feet away. Certainly they could have seen the outlines of the horse hidden among the saplings and pinned helpless there, but they had no time for a sideward glance. They were too busy closing in toward the center.

Bull Hunter waited until these too had passed out of sight, and then he sent Diablo out of the thicket, cantering straight back toward the Dunbar ranch.

CHAPTER XVI

A KNIGHT-ERRANT

IT had been Mary Hood who heard the cry: "Bull Hunter is here, up to some deviltry. Everybody out!" And it was she who stood on the veranda, dressed in white, and looked down to the giant, as he waved his hat.

When the hunt swept after the fugitive, into the forest behind the stables, she ran up to a top window of the big house. Here, with a pair of field glasses, she followed the chase across the rolling ground, her heart leaping involuntarily in sympathy with the magnificent black and his endangered rider. When they disappeared, even Hal Dunbar, far to the rear, his gray laboring under the weight of his big master, she turned from the window and went thoughtfully down to her own room.

She was remembering that first day when Bull Hunter came to the house of Dunbar, a mighty man indeed, as tall as Hal Dunbar and as bulky, with an even greater suggestion of muscular power. To most people he seemed inhumanly large, but the girl, accustomed all her life to the gigantic Dunbar, looked on the size of Bull Hunter as a more or less common thing.

As she recalled it, the stranger on that first day had talked like a child, simply and directly; but Hal Dunbar had told her that Hunter was a snake in the grass; and before the stranger left the house, he had shot down her father, the redoubtable Jack Hood, and left him dangerously wounded. That made him the mortal enemy, not only of Jack Hood but of all the Dunbars, for Jack Hood was something more than a mere foreman of the great ranch. He had directed it for half his life, his daughter was the prospective wife of Hal, the young owner, and Jack Hood himself was really an integral part of the owner's household.

Yet, thinking of the stranger, she found that she did not hate him as she should. No matter how terrible he might be to men, she felt that she could control him by as small a thing as the lifting of her finger. There was even something horrible in the way in which the Dunbar men had rushed out at the first appearance of the poor fellow, like a pack of wolves.

By this time perhaps, he was dead; or his death would come certainly before noon, since no one man could be expected to escape from so many hard riders. And at his death——

At this point in her reflections a deep, smooth bass voice, outside the house, cut in on her thoughts: "Mary Hood! Oh, Mary Hood!"

And she knew, though she had only heard that voice on one occasion, that it was Bull Hunter who called. She ran to the window. There he stood, tall and mighty, beside the shining stallion. He was unchanged, only a little leaner and harder and more tanned of face, a trifle more alert in carriage.

She looked on him with a shrinking of the heart, as if he were a ghost of the broad daylight. She had seen him, it seemed, only a moment before, riding across the rolling pasture lands, with the stream of hunters behind him, and now he stood here alone. She rubbed her eyes; the vision persisted.

"Mary Hood!" he was calling again. "Oh, Mary Hood!"

The madman! Did he not know that if there were one able-bodied man in the house, he would be shot down like a dog if that call were heard? Lucky for him that every soul had taken to the saddle for the hunt! And then, remembering that she was alone in the place, she trembled with a new fear. But only for a moment, and then she was calm again. She went boldly to the window and leaned out a little.

He saw her at once and, for a moment, stared up without speaking. Then he dragged off his sombrero, leaving his hair wild and blowing. It was more than an act of courtesy. There was a touch of worship in the gesture and in the uplifted face that made her uneasy. Then he raised a locket on a chain.

"I have brought back to you," he said, "something that was taken from your father."

And for this he had been hunted away like a mad dog! She cried out one grateful word and then hurried downstairs, through the big house and onto the veranda. There she paused a moment.

Seen from the level he was larger than from above, and since she had first known him, there had come into his face that wild, uneasy look which she had noted, once or twice before, in outcasts of the mountains. He was holding up the locket and smiling. No matter what he had done, no matter if he had killed every one of the men who had hunted him, she had no cause to fear him. She went down the steps from the veranda very slowly and crossed the terrace. When she had taken the locket she drew back in surprise at the temerity which had led her to face this man alone.

"I took it from the man who stole it from your father," he said simply. "I knew that you would be unhappy without it."

He talked slowly to the girl, picking his words. With Pete Reeve he used the rough language of the cow-punchers, but the girl appealed in a different way, and there was enough knowledge of good English in him to enable him to respond.

"They shall all know about it," she answered. "They shall all know why you came here, to be driven away like a dog! But how did you break through them? And if you fought my father——"

"There was no fight. I ran away from them and hid and then came back."

A quiet way of stating a remarkable fact, for how could one man hide from twenty, on ground which the twenty knew like the pages of a book? But she felt at once that he could never be induced to talk about his personal exploits. She found herself smiling at him with a new liking.

"It was so lucky that the thief—I mean your friend——" She found herself involved in a hope-less mess of words. Of course the thief was some partner of Bull Hunter's.

"He is a thief," said Bull, "but he is not my friend. I am an honest man—so far."

At least he had taken no offense; but she knew

that she was crimson. She could tell it by the wonder with which the big man searched her face.

He went on talking to spare her embarrassment. "Because I knew him well enough to learn he had this locket in his possession, you thought he was my friend. But even if I live with thieves, I am not a thief, Mary Hood."

"Of course you aren't. And I——"

"I didn't care anything about the locket when he first showed it to me," he continued, "until I saw the face—it is very like you." He paused a moment. "It was hard for me to bring it back."

"You have done so much to bring a mere locket back to me?" she asked, thrilling at the thought of it. "And, besides the long journey, to face all of Hal's men——"

He broke in as she paused, and he was frowning in his honesty and bewilderment as to the choice of words. "It isn't just to bring you the locket," he went on. "I wanted to see you a lot, and I wanted to see you smile, perhaps, when you took the locket. I guess that's the chief reason."

She was somewhere between blushing and laughter at his painful simplicity.

"Otherwise," he continued, "I could have found some one else to take it back, some one who wouldn't have been in any danger from your friends. So you see what I have done has been quite bad. It made so many men ride so hard."

He waved toward the direction in which the posse had ridden and smiled apologetically at her. She thought at first that there must be hidden sarcasm in the speech, but apparently he was as downright as the broad day. So, far from expecting gratitude, he was actually beginning to ask pardon for what he had done.

"Do you dare stay one minute longer?" she asked suddenly.

"Ten minutes, if you will let me."

"They may come back."

"Perhaps."

She smiled with pleasure at his calmness. "You're a rare fellow, Charlie Hunter," she told him. "How long have you ridden this trail?"

"Three days."

"Three days, to bring me this? There isn't another person like you in the world! I'll never forget it."

He shook his head, unhappy at this outburst of eulogy. "There is one very strange thing to-day," he said to change the subject. "First I come, and twenty men take guns and horses and ride out to meet me. I come again, and there is only one girl without a weapon. You are strange people in this place, Mary Hood!"

She had been Mary all her life, and there was something novel and very pleasant in the use of both names together. It endowed her, it seemed, with a new and more unique personality.

"Then we should get along very well," she replied with a smile, "for you are certainly strange among men, Charlie Hunter."

"Yes," he said judicially, "I think I could teach you to like me. I have taught a horse and a wild dog, you see."

She laughed at the comparison. "A wild horse and a wild dog?"

"The dog left me because of another man. But Diablo, you see, is my friend."

"And gentle?"

"As a lamb."

She stretched out her hand; the black stallion sprang far away.

"Gentle!" she exclaimed.

"He has to be introduced," explained Bull. "Now come with me."

He went to Diablo and laid a hand on his neck. The black acknowledged the caress with a quick pricking of his ears and then flattened them again and regarded the timid approach of the girl with angry eyes.

"He's ready to jump at me!" she declared and stopped.

"He will not. Come slowly—steady, Diablo!— and with your hand out. Touch his nose. If you do that once, he'll remember you, I think."

"Unless he chooses to bite my hand off."

"He will not stir while I talk to him. You see?"

He began to talk smoothly and softly, and the ears of the stallion flickered and came forward, even though Mary began to come close again. Between fear and anger at her coming and pleasure at the soft voice of the master, he trembled from head to foot.

Mary Hood was very much afraid, yet she came slowly up until her outstretched hand touched the nose of the stallion. He snorted and winced like a wild horse, when the weight of a man first settles on his back, but though his lips twitched, he made no effort to snap.

"Talk to him," said Bull.

Then she talked, as only those who love horses know how. Bull Hunter left the side of the stallion, and Diablo remained motionless, sniffing the hand of the girl.

"And is this the way you always introduce people to him?" she asked when she turned at last to the big man.

"You are the first; perhaps you are the last. It has made me always happy to be the only one who can go near Diablo, but to-day, I don't know why, it seems to me that I am happier to share him with some one. See, he is following you!"

"No, he is going to you. You're right! You're right! He is coming after me!" She turned and patted the beautiful head of Diablo in delight. "You are a wizard with horses. A true wizard!" she assured him.

"I love them," said Bull Hunter. "That is all. Besides——" He stopped and raised his head. The wind was freshening out of the north, and now it carried to them the sound of a neigh, then the beat of hoofs, far, far away, but distinguishable in the thin mountain air. "They are coming back," said Bull Hunter sadly, "and I must go."

The girl turned angrily toward the approaching sound. Then she touched the arm of Bull Hunter. "You must go, my friend. They have no right to hunt you, but people do not stand on right and wrong on this ranch. I know you have done nothing wrong. You fought my father fairly, and it was his own fault that the fight came at all. I've heard of it all! But now you must go quickly! I shall never forget you and Diablo, but go now!"

He nodded, admitting the gloomy necessity, and

yet he still lingered, hunting for words to fit an idea which had just come to him. "There is only one thing more," he said. "I shall miss the locket, Mary Hood, more than you can understand."

"What do you mean?"

"There are lonely times in the mountains, you see. There are times so lonely that a picture is just like another person. It is company. You understand?"

There was no mystery in it. A child would have known. His worship of her was in his eyes, and the girl flushed, pitying him, and excited and proud of the tribute. "Of all the strange men who have ever lived," she said, "you are the strangest. You have ridden three days and risked being shot in order to ask me if you can keep a picture?"

"In order to give you the picture and ask it back from your hands," he corrected her. "That is very different. I can find anybody's picture and keep it, but that gives me no right. You see, that painter was very cunning. He put a smile on your face that might be because you were very happy with a friend, or riding a horse, or dreaming, and if you give me the picture, Mary Hood, when I look at it I shall feel that you may at that very moment be thinking of me. That is simple, but it means a great deal to me. Will you let me have it?"

She dropped it into his hand. "You have earned it a thousand times over, and it makes me proud to have you want it." The outburst of frankness left her afraid that she had said too much. But Bull Hunter was too busy examining the locket and putting it away to notice her confusion.

"It is not to be a gift," he declared. "You may

want something done, somewhere, somehow. Let me do it in exchange for this."

She nodded, smilingly excited again; and all the time she wondered that this big, simple fellow could amuse her so much and give her a peculiar uplifted feeling. It was a novel idea, this purchase by service. It was a scheme worthy of the old days of knight-errantry, and naturally she thought of jousts and battles. Then the inspiration struck her that was to give her many a headache before all was done.

"Charlie Hunter," she said, "if you want to earn the locket find the man who stole it and turn him over to the law. Would you do as much as that?"

As she turned, the slant sun of the young morning glinted in her eyes, blinding her, so that she did not see the sudden change in his expression.

"Mary Hood," he answered after a little pause, "I've sat by the camp fire with that man, and I've eaten his bacon and bread."

The disappointment made her sigh.

"But if you want him taken——"

"I do!"

"Then," said Bull Hunter, "I'll do my best. Good-by. Perhaps I shall see you again!"

He was on his horse before she was able to answer: "But of course I'll see you again!"

"Who knows?" answered Charlie Hunter from the back of Diablo. "There are always two ways a man trail may end."

Leaving her breathless, he touched the flank of Diablo with his heel, and the great black swept him down the terraces.

CHAPTER XVII

THE GHOST'S PROGRESS

MEANWHILE the great wolf dog, The Ghost, more wolf indeed than dog, had fled through the night without pause. In his mind all was a sad jumble. He had fled from the call of his master for a good and definite reason. He had seen clearly from the beginning that it was the will of the master that he become kind to men and the creatures of men.

That scent, which he loathed and dreaded the most, the scent of man, so keen in the wind and so strong under foot, making the hair of all beasts of prey prickle and ruff up, that very scent, according to the apparent will of the master, was the thing which should make The Ghost kindly to those who possessed it. Their servants he must not kill; themselves he must regard with awe.

Therefore he fled through the night at his best long-distance pace. He discovered ere long that his muscles were not what they had once been. He had done no real running in the company of Bull Hunter. To one who could kill, eat full, sleep, and do an easy fifty miles, all within the space of twenty-four hours, what was a paltry thirty miles a day, at the end of which he was fed by the master? The pads of his feet were soft. His wind was not sound. The story of the trail, told in a hundred and a thousand scents, was dim and often almost

illegible, for his nostrils had been clogged and dulled
by the soot of camp fires. Decidedly he was not
his old self.

One thing was certain: The dogs would not
accept him, and Bull Hunter would not accept the
wolves. Between wolf and man he must take his
choice, and he hunted now for his kind. Many
a word came to his nostrils of rabbit and chip-
munk and birds and coyotes and foxes, and once he
followed for half a dozen miles a promising scent,
only to find at the end of the trail a little prairie
wolf which fled madly at his coming.

The Ghost turned upwind in disgust from such a
quarry. He gave himself a mile or two of terrific
running to make him forget the shame of his
mistake, and at the end of it, without warning scent,
he dropped suddenly upon the thing he sought.

Half a dozen lobos fed on the carcass of two
new-slain calves, in which the life was still hot.
The moon was a dim sickle cutting through the
trees on the peak above. By its uncertain light
The Ghost viewed his fellows and was glad at heart.
He dropped upon his haunches and gave voice to
the hunting call which had more than once passed,
wailing and shivering, through the mountains and
made apprehensive ranchers reach for their rifles and
curse the darkness which screened the marauder.
But far better was it known to the other big loafer
wolves. More than one had felt his teeth, and
there were few of the others who had not seen
him fight. One bay was enough to send the six
wolves in the hollow, leaping away from their meat,
apprehensive and on the alert.

The Ghost looked on with immense satisfaction,

and having stared his full and seen that not one
of the band dared go back to its food, until his
orders were known, he dropped down into the hollow
at a lazy jog trot.

When he came near he saw that there were three
youngsters, two females and a scarred old veteran
of a leader. Few loafer wolves could gather a
pack to themselves, but this one-eared hero, in his
strength and wisdom, had proved the exception.
He made a pace forward from his companions as
The Ghost came to a halt over the first carcass and
stared about him. But the forward step of the leader
was not a challenge. It was merely a feeble attempt
to assert his dignity in the eyes of his followers,
and knowing that, The Ghost despised a fight which
would have been murder. Besides, he was too wise
to battle for pleasure, knowing full well that the
weakest yearling wolf may ruin the fiercest of his
elders by a lucky bite that severs a tendon.

However, it was well to assert his mastery, even
with the weak. It might be his pleasure to lead
this pack, and, if that proved to be his will, he
might as well begin now. A hungry yearling ventured toward the second carcass. The Ghost sent
him back with a terrible snarl. Only the veteran
of many a wild fight could know the art of such
a snarl. The yearling leaped back with his tail
between his legs, and The Ghost sauntered carelessly
toward the body of the second dead calf.

He had barely reached it when a low-pitched snarl
from the old leader made him stop, quivering. For
that whining snarl of fear and rage meant, in wolf
talk, man. The Ghost jerked his head to one side,
but the wind carried to his nostrils only the pure

scent of the grass and the trees. He glanced back at the others and started in astonishment.

They had formed in a loose semicircle, "One Ear" in the center, with a female on either side, and on the flanks were the yearlings. They moved slowly forward, crouching low to the ground, with necks and heads stretched straight out, their noses pointing toward him; and now from every throat came that same whining snarl which meant man.

The Ghost glared in astonishment. Was it possible that they were about to attack him en masse, as wolves attack a dog? He settled back as if for a leap, and at once the six divided and crouched lower, but they still advanced. He sent his longest and greatest hunting cry, ringing and filling the hollow. But though they paused until the last echo died away, the advance began again the next moment.

Then he understood. It was the scent of man that lingered on him. More than that perhaps, he had learned from his society with man the ways of a dog. With fear and rage The Ghost watched that silent advance of his fellows.

Suddenly one of the she-wolves coughed and darted at him to catch his flank. The Ghost sprang high and far. His aim was not the she-wolf, but the cunning old leader who had kept discreetly in the background. High over him sprang The Ghost. It was a trick he had learned in his youth in a battle with a terrible old wolfhound, which nearly cost him his life, for the hound had the art of vaulting above an enemy and snapping as he shot by, an improvement on the old wolf method of cutting from the side.

It worked now like a charm. The teeth of The

Ghost sank into the back of One Ear's neck, and the shock spun The Ghost straight over in mid-air, before his teeth tore loose, yet he landed on his feet, and he landed running. To make one attack in the face of any odds was the part of valor. To run with all his might from six hostile members of his own kind was the part of extreme wisdom, and The Ghost was wise.

The yearlings, who are sprinters par excellence, nearly caught him in the first two hundred yards, but after that he drew smoothly away. One Ear himself was too badly hurt to follow, and the she-wolves quickly lost interest. In a mile the pursuit ended, and The Ghost drew down his pace to the tireless lope.

He had escaped a great danger, he had inflicted a severe wound without return, and that, in the wolf code, is the greatest happiness. But in spite of his triumph, the heart of The Ghost was aching. He had been outcast by his brothers!

He reached the buildings of a squatter a few miles farther on, pitifully small sheds in the midst of the wilderness of mountains. Here, in a little outer corral, he found a sleek young two-year-old colt asleep. The Ghost leaped the fence and then paused to grin at the simplicity of the thing. It needed only one soft growl to waken the colt and bring him in terror to his feet, still blind with sleep. Then he could dive under and cut the throat of the horse with a bite.

Pausing to enjoy the thing in prospect, The Ghost cleansed his fur, then circled the colt slowly. The stupid creature was so deep in sleep that The Ghost could sniff within a fraction of an inch of his

hide without alarming him. And still he delayed
the snarl that was to rouse the victim for the
slaughter. He sat down on his haunches with lolling tongue and pondered. It was strange, this
reluctance to kill. Continually in the back of his
brain was the thought of black Diablo and the
many games that they had played together. Of
course it had been most perfect when the master
had played with them. He knew how to direct the
game. In truth those had been happy days!

But he was an outcast from them. He had fled
from the master's voice, and having once offended,
he would never be accepted again. Even so, he
was also an outcast from the society of other wolves.
Then what place remained to him?

He started up to make the kill, and, as he did
so, the colt raised his head and looked idly about
him. It was a head very like the head of Diablo,
when The Ghost had slipped out into the corral on
many a night to touch noses with the stallion, and
while he was crouched for the spring, The Ghost
felt his muscles relax.

At length, as noiselessly as he had come, he slipped
from the corral and fled away across the hills.

It was the beginning of a period of ceaseless
wandering. He killed irregularly, joylessly, only for
food. Neither did it matter what was his prey,
but more and more there was a growing distaste
for the creatures of man. Now he caught squirrels
and chipmunks and rabbits, beggarly prey for The
Ghost as he had once been. But, alas, he was
changed! There was one single instant of joy,
a battle with a lone veteran of a wolf whom he
met on a narrow trail along a cañon side. That

fight ended with his foe toppling a thousand feet below to destruction, and The Ghost went on.

One who watched him would have known that he was hunting; but of that The Ghost was unaware. He only knew that his heart ached steadily, that his muscles were growing lean and his skin was hanging in folds, for it was the old tragedy of the wilderness. Wild creatures which have been once tamed can never be truly wild again; the chain with which men hold their slaves has no weight. It is the mind, and this chain can never be broken.

While The Ghost hunted for happiness in the mountains where he had been a king, roaming in great and ever widening circles, chance brought him the explanation which he himself could never have arrived at, for, as he lay under a tree one day, a dust cloud, far down a winding trail, dissolved into a horseman; and when the horseman drew near, he saw the glint of the sun on the shining black charger. Then a veering of the wind brought him an old, old scent.

The Ghost leaped to his feet. There was something like a great thirst in his throat, and yet the coldest, clearest water that ever bubbled in a mountain spring could never have satisfied it. Presently he sat back on his haunches, and the long, weird, heart-chilling wolf yell went echoing down the mountainside.

In response the sun flashed on a naked rifle barrel, as the rider swung it into place. The Ghost winced away. Well he knew the meaning of that glimmer of steel, wavering back and forth in a straight line that steadied to a point. Yet he knew the hand on the gun also, and he rose mournfully and raised his head to wait for the end. Twice, blinking at that point of light on the barrel, as the rider drew the bead, he thought the end had come; and then the rifle was lowered, and the hand of the man went up.

A voice was calling him down the wind, a voice that made his heart thunder in response. The Ghost fled like the wind to meet Bull Hunter. Three swift circles he made around the horse and rider, with Diablo whinnying a soft welcome, and then he ran to them and placed his forepaws on the knee of the master and licked his hand.

He knew that the other hand stroked his battle-scarred head, while the voice, speaking as kindly as ever, was saying to him: "Old Pete Reeve was right. You're like him, partner. You're no dog, and you're no wolf, but you belong in between. Just where, darned if I know, but you and me'll work it out together. If only I could do the same for Pete!"

CHAPTER XVIII

THE CHALLENGE

IT was far north on the mountain desert, in one of those towns which grow up like weeds and die like weeds in the West, according as lumber and mining camps are opened and closed and as the cattle centers change.

Viewed by the hawk's eye from above, the town was merely a rough collection of shacks, whose roofs sent back the sunshine in a myriad of heat waves. The houses were weathered to the color of the desert, a deadly drab. Some of them had been painted once or twice, but dry heat in summer and fierce storms in winter peeled up the paint and soaked it away. It was not a town in the desert; it was part of the desert, called by grace a town, yet to its inhabitants it was a haven of refuge. Under those low roofs was shade, and the floors could be doused with water many times a day for the sake of coolness.

Dunkin and Pete Reeve sat on the veranda, freshly drenched from buckets, and each took his ease, tilted far back in a chair, the soles of his feet braced against separate pillars. In that position the hotel proprietor found them as he came sweating up the steps.

"When I asked for the hotel mail," said he, "the postmaster give me this letter for you, Mr. Hardy."

Then he passed on into the hotel. As for Hardy,

alias Dunkin, he sat as one stunned, turning the letter over and over in his hands.

"But it can't be for me," he declared to Reeve. "Must be some other John Hardy around here, a real one, I mean. Nobody that would write to me knows I'm here."

"It's meant for you, right enough," Reeve assured him. "If there was another Hardy around here wouldn't they know about him? Open up and let's hear the good news."

Dunkin, still shaking his head, opened the letter and read aloud:

"I've been looking for you a long time, Dunkin, and just the other day a gent blew into town and told me about a fellow named Hardy. What he said tallied pretty closely with you; and when he spoke about Pete Reeve, I was sure it was you.

"So I'm writing this letter to let you know why I want to see you. For reasons I can't explain, it's come to the point where one of us has to go down, and naturally I'd rather that one should be you. I don't care how you want to fight, on horses or foot, or with rifles or Colts or knives.

"I'm over in Tuckertown now, the eighteenth, and I'll wait here till the morning of the day after to-morrow. If you don't come looking for me by that time I'll come looking for you.

"Say hello to Pete Reeve for me.
                              "CHARLES HUNTER."

Dunkin finished the letter in a staggering voice. Then he laughed, crumpled it up, threw it on the floor, picked it up and unraveled the tangle of paper again, and finally launched a stream of tremendous curses.

"I'll go to Tuckertown for him," he said at length. "And when I get through with him, there won't be enough left to fill a coffeepot. But what's happened to him? Has he gone crazy?"

"He always hated you," said Pete Reeve with a surprising lack of emotion.

"Say, I think you're on his side."

"Sure I am, except that he's hunting you, while you and me happen to be partners, and the law of the range stands that a gent has to back up his partner. No, Dunkin, if Bull comes for you, while you and me are on the trail, he'll have to drop both of us in order to get one."

"Thanks," said Dunkin, "but I don't need no help. I'll settle the business of this gent in a jiffy. After I say one word the buzzards can finish the sentence."

He enjoyed his own little joke so hugely that he almost laughed himself back into a good humor. But he came out of his laughter sharply, and, rising from the chair, he said: "He's waiting for me. Want to come along to Tuckertown and see the party?"

"The party is more like to come off right here," said Reeve gravely. "This is the twentieth, and he's due to come. His letter must have got hung up in the mails some way. It's only eight miles to Tuckertown."

"Why did he write, the fool? Why not come over like a man and give me a dare? I've always hated him, too!"

"Even a snake gives you a rattle before he hits

you," said Reeve. "Bull wanted to give you fair warning of what was coming. And if I was you, Dunkin, I'd take that warning and start riding."

"I'm not afraid of him," replied Dunkin. "You say he's pretty good with a gun, but you think everything he does is pretty good. Well, I'll give him a try. What you say about Bull Hunter don't count."

"Maybe not," assented the withered little man. "He's the best friend I've got, the best friend any man could have. He'd give his life for me. That's why I want you to run for it, Dunkin. If you stay, I got to stay with you and face my old partner with a gun. If you run, I'll run with you and show you a way to get off, for a while, anyway."

"For a while? You talk like this gent Hunter was sure to get me."

"He is," answered Reeve with the same disconcerting calm. "In spite of you and in spite of me he'll probably get you, if it takes him ten years for the job. Dunkin, take another think and put a saddle on your hoss and go."

There was something so convincing in Reeve's manner of speaking that Dunkin actually started across the veranda, but he halted after a few steps and turned back. "I'll see him hung first," he declared at length. "Here we are in the only part of the range where you ain't known, and where we can work with a free hand. I won't be turned out by any thick-head like Hunter. Reeve, we're going to stick, that's final. If you want to give me a hand agin' this gent, I'll say pretty frank that I'll be glad to have you. If you don't want to help, I'll stay and face him alone."

Reeve made a gesture of surrender. "I've told you what I'll do already," he said, "and I stick by that. But I'd rather be dead myself than shoot a bullet at Hunter!"

He had hardly made up his mind when a boy, riding bareback on a fleet pony, dashed down the street and ran to the veranda with a scared face. "They's a gent coming with a wolf!" he called to them. "A gent with an honest-injun loafer wolf trotting along in front of him."

It brought Pete Reeve and Dunkin to their feet.

"He's here," whispered Dunkin. "Are you with me, Pete?"

"I'm with you. But the wolf? Has The Ghost come back to him?"

"Must be, because—yes, that's The Ghost!"

Around the bend of the single street glided the gray form of the big lobo. He paused with head erect, the broad wistful face turning inquiringly to either side. Then, from behind, came the master on the tall black stallion, and The Ghost moved on. The strange little procession brought people to windows and doors, staring in amazement tinged with fear. More than one man reached for his gun at the sight of the wolf dog; and just across the street from the hotel, a woman scolded her children hastily back into the house.

Straight to the veranda of the hotel came The Ghost, reared and placed his forepaws on the edge of the porch and stared long and earnestly into the face of Dunkin. It was as though he had picked out by foreknowledge the enemy of his master, though doubtless Bull Hunter had taught him the scent of the enemy. Then the great animal slipped down and returned like a silent shadow to his master.

By this time Hunter had seen them. He halted his horse and turned in the saddle toward them.

"Now," said Dunkin, his whole body trembling with nervous anxiety, "now I'll make my play!"

"If you do, it's murder," said Reeve. "Bull Hunter won't make a gun play in this town full of people, and he don't expect you to try. Look! He's waving to us. If he meant quick action, d'you think he'd take his hand that far away from his gun? Never in the world."

Bull shouted a cheery greeting to them and then swung out of the saddle and strode toward them. If he had looked huge in the saddle, he seemed more mountainous than ever, walking on foot. Diablo followed at his heels like a dog.

Pete Reeve ran to meet him and wrung his hands. He looked like a midget before the giant, yet if any man of the mountain desert had been asked to pick the more formidable of the two, he would have picked the midget without a moment's hesitation, for at this time in his career, Bull Hunter was known to be huge, but very little else was widely known about him; while the fame of Pete Reeve had spread far and wide.

They walked on together toward the veranda, laughing happily. At the veranda they met Dunkin, and the laughter stopped.

"I sent you a letter," said Bull Hunter mildly, "asking you to come to meet me in Tuckertown. But I guess the letter didn't come, Dunkin."

"It come, right enough," answered Dunkin. "And

I'm ready to meet you anywhere. The only reason I didn't come was because you ain't worth that much trouble, Bull. Besides, the letter just got here. It must have been held up. For the rest, I've hated the sight of you for a long time, and I'm glad we're going to have it out now. Mighty glad!"

"I'm not," answered Bull. "I've never liked you, Dunkin, but I've never hated you."

"Only enough to want to pump me full of lead, eh?" asked the robber.

"Lead? Shooting?" asked Bull in mild surprise. "Why, man, I'm not going to kill or try to kill you."

"You ain't? Then what is it that you aim to try to do with me?"

"Take you alive and turn you over to the law. That's my job."

It brought a gasp from both Reeve and Dunkin.

"Son," said Dunkin hotly, "you got one chance in three of dropping me with a bullet in a fair fight; but you nor nobody else has got a chance in a million of taking me alive!"

"Maybe I ain't," answered Bull mildly, "but I'll die trying it."

"And while you're trying," went on Dunkin coldly, "remember that you got two on your hands, not one. When you get me you got to get Pete Reeve first."

It was a thunderbolt to Bull Hunter. He made a gesture like a blind man toward the little gun fighter.

"Pete," he exclaimed, "are you with him in this?"

Pete Reeve dropped his head. "It's an old law," he said bitterly, "and it always has to work. I'm on the trail with Dunkin, Bull. In a month or two I may be away from him, and then you're free to tackle him alone. But while I'm with him, my grub is his grub and my hoss is his hoss and my gun is his gun. That's the way it works, and that's the way it's always got to work, or else they'll be no more living in the West. I guess that's the straight of it."

"That may be the way with you," said Bull Hunter, "but no matter where I was I'd never lift a hand agin' you. Not for love or money, Pete. It changes things a good deal." He went a half step closer to Dunkin. "There's one thing new I got to tell you, Dunkin. I started out wanting just to take you alive. I'm beginning to want to kill you, and I'm beginning to think I will."

His broad forehead wrinkled with thought. "I'd forgive any man a lot, but never the one that turned Pete Reeve agin' me. Dunkin, watch yourself. I'm going to foller you and Pete, when you leave town. I'm going to watch my chance. I'll wait maybe a year, but I'll get you away from Pete and tie you like a bale of hay and take you to town to the sheriff. Keep that in your head, my friend!"

Dunkin attempted to sneer, but his lips trembled beyond control. He tried to laugh, but the sound dried up in his throat. Then Bull Hunter turned on his heel and strode away, the thick dust of the street squirting up like steam from the heavy stamping of his feet.

CHAPTER XIX

LOSS AND GAIN

THAT night after supper the spirits of Dunkin rose perceptibly. "It's all bluff, Pete," he said to his companion, as he lighted a cigarette after the big tin cup of coffee that finished his meal. "If Hunter meant business he'd have stayed right here and watched us till we left town. But he's disappeared. It's all bluff. When he seen that you were with me he lost his nerve."

"Not if ten like me were with you," answered the imperturbable Reeve. "He's cached himself away in some shack near the town, and he's watching the trails from there. But there's one way we might give him the slip. He probably doesn't expect us to move away from town for a couple of days. If we make a jump in the middle of to-night we might take him by surprise and get by."

Dunkin glanced twice at his friend to make sure that he was serious. The idea of Pete Reeve stealing away by night from any man alive was not in the books, but there was no doubting the seriousness of the little man.

"You know this gent a pile better than I do," said Dunkin at last. "So you run the party, and I'll do what you say."

Accordingly they went to sleep early, with orders to be awakened a little after midnight. At that hour they were up and in the saddle. There could not have been a better night for a secret escape; there could not have been a worse night for travel. A chill wind was coming down from the higher northern mountains, carrying a piercing drizzle of rain, and, though their slickers turned the force of it, it found crevices here and there, and the sharp wind drove the rain to the skin.

Dunkin steadily cursed the weather and Bull Hunter, and twice he begged the little man to turn back with him to the hotel and bid defiance to the giant, but Reeve was inflexible in his purpose.

"If we get over the trail of the Culver Pass," said he, "we'll be in country that Hunter doesn't know, and he'll be at sea. Keep that hoss moving!"

So they plodded steadily over the road which the rain was quickly turning to slush. They drifted down the main street to the outer limits of the town, unseen and unheard, for the drum of rain on the roofs covered all minor sounds.

In the open country the rain was merely a swishing sound on the sand and dead grass. The air was filled with the scent of the arid soil, as it greedily drank up the moisture, and there were steady, whispering noises like promises of the green life that was to come. By the road, just outside the village, they passed some low clumps of shrubbery.

"Suppose he were lying out in there?" suggested Pete Reeve. "If he was he'd see us pass quick enough."

"Too low to cover a man as big as him," said Dunkin confidently. "Besides, nobody but a crazy man would lie out in this rain. Pete, you're all wrong about this. We don't need to hurry. Bull

Hunter is asleep and snoring. We're just fading out, and he'll never find us beyond the Culver Pass."

"I'll believe that when we're safely over," answered Pete with unshaken gloom.

Indeed, at that very moment there was a watcher in the shrubbery who heard their voices. Not a man, but a great wolf dog crouched under a bush that formed an almost perfect tent above him to shed the rain. As the two horsemen passed he glided across the road to the leeward side and skulked swiftly from bush to bush, taking the scent.

Presently he appeared to be satisfied and shot back toward the town. The town itself was not his goal, however, but skirting around behind it, with the sand scuffing up behind him from his hurrying paws, he came to a wretched group of trees on the far side of the village and close to the trail where it entered the town. Among these trees he plunged and came presently on the great bulk of Hunter, sitting with his back against a tree, wrapped in a capacious slicker. All night he had kept patient watch, and now the cold nose of the wolf dog touched his hand.

As he turned his head, The Ghost retreated, looking back over his shoulder. At that the master rose hastily, flung a saddle on Diablo, and was instantly under way.

His stratagem had been simple enough. In the shed behind the hotel he had taken the wolf to the horses of Reeve and Dunkin to freshen their scent in his nose. Then at dark he posted the big animal on the far side of the town. He himself guarded the only other way of entering or leaving the town. He could trust The Ghost to report. Many a time before he had used the cunning hunting instincts of the loafer wolf and taught him to play his very game of tag with Pete Reeve. Now it stood him in good stead.

They went at a mild trot through the village, but as soon as they hit the open trail beyond he gave a short whistle that sent The Ghost bounding away in the lead, to disappear instantly behind the thick curtain of night and the rain; he himself let Diablo take his head for a burst of strong running, until a figure shot into view again. It was The Ghost returning to apprise his master that he had located the fugitives and was keeping in touch with them.

As he returned, The Ghost gamboled about the rider, leaping high and snapping in pretended ferocity at the nose of Diablo, for this game of hunting was the greatest joy in The Ghost's life with his master. Playing it, he had a faint taste of the old free days when he was king of the mountains, and there was almost an added joy in playing it with Bull Hunter, for when he ran a quarry to the ground, were it grizzly or mountain lion, the rifle of the master was always sure to make the kill. Odds ceased to exist, and, with the master in sight, The Ghost would have attacked at command a whole host of lions.

His task this night was far simpler; it was ridiculously easy for him. As the connecting link he raced back and forth, coming just within hearing of the splash of water and mud under the feet of the horses of the fugitives, and then loping back to communicate news of his industry. One word was all the reward he wanted.

Sometimes he stopped to touch noses with Diablo;

sometimes he took a brief vacation, and racing through some neighboring field or wood, he made short detours along the scents of wet trails, not yet drowned, then back to play the game for his master.

Of course it was invaluable to Bull Hunter to have this assistant spy. He himself could linger far behind entirely out of danger of being heard or seen by the men he trailed. As he rode along, secure on the back of Diablo, even when the trail became most treacherous, he tried to order some plan of attack.

It was by no means simple. To attack Dunkin alone would have been nothing; to attack him and try to take him alive was a thousand times more difficult and necessitated a surprise. But to surprise him while Pete Reeve rode in his company was practically impossible.

The rain ceased while he was in the midst of these reflections. The northern wind, which had blown the storm upon them, was succeeded by a brisk western breeze which whipped the sky clean of clouds in a few moments and left the big mountains and the stars and the blue-black depths of the sky above him, while all around there was a crinkling sound of the thirsty earth, drinking. It also meant that Bull Hunter could see his surroundings more clearly.

They were rapidly climbing toward the heart of that narrow defile known as the Culver Pass. The trail that wound through it sometimes climbed along the side of the cliff, with barely enough room for one horseman. The cliffs themselves dropped down to the bed of the swift torrent which had cut the gulch. Ordinarily a trail would have been made on the bank of the stream itself. But it was impossible to travel over the enormous boulders which were strewn on either side of the water, and the trail was forced to follow a very precarious course.

It would be impossible to attack the two who rode in front on such a trail, for they were probably in single file, with the redoubtable Pete Reeve himself in the rear, to guard against precisely such an attack. Yet it was very necessary to stop the two before they got out of the pass and reached the broken country beyond, a bad stretch through which pursuit would be very difficult, if not impossible.

Bull Hunter reviewed his means of attack. There was the rifle slung in the holster; there was the heavy revolver at his hip. But neither was really available if he hoped to take Dunkin alive. There was also the lariat, and that, in a way, was a weapon of another sort and precisely adapted to such a capture. With that thought the idea came to Bull Hunter.

He put Diablo at the first slope which he reached, leading toward the summit of the cliff upon that side. It was a desperate climb. The Ghost went on ahead, pointing the way in the most effectual manner possible, for he knew intimately the capacities of Diablo when it came to climbing, and he scouted on, exploring every dangerous slope and coming back to show the way up the easiest course. Even then Bull Hunter could not stay in the saddle and hope to make the climb. He had to dismount before they had gone a hundred yards.

A little farther on it was necessary to remove the saddle from Diablo. Bull Hunter toiled and moiled up the wet hill, carrying the heavy saddle, and Diablo struggled valiantly in his wake, with The Ghost as the vanguard.

Finally, as the gray dawn appeared, they reached the crest. Hunter saddled again in frantic haste. It had taken incredibly long to make that short climb; but looking down into the dizzy shadows of the cañon, he wondered how he had made it at all. Perhaps the fugitives would have got out of Culver Pass by this time and were already riding into the comparative safety of the bad lands beyond.

But there was an immediate reward for the climb. The surface of the crest was a long stretch of almost level plateau. It was impossible to ride at more than a walk along the trail by the cañon. Up here a horse could run at full gallop, and Bull put Diablo to his full speed, with the wind turned to a gale in his face by the rush of his flight.

One gesture told The Ghost what his part in the business must be. He rushed on ahead, swinging along the verge of the drop toward the gulch and scanning the trail as it wound along the cliff. With anxiety Bull Hunter noted that the wolf dog still kept running on at full speed, though the end of the pass had almost come. He was beginning to despair when The Ghost changed his lope to a slouching trot, hanging his nose close to the edge of the cliff. The dog had found them, and the heart of Bull Hunter leaped again.

He took Diablo in a wide detour, so that the sound of the galloping might not come to the two on the narrow cliff trail, and swinging in ahead of The Ghost again he flung himself from the saddle, whipped the lariat from its place and ran to a point of vantage.

It was a point where the cliff jagged out in a triangle, and the trail followed that conformation in an elbow bend. There had been more than one tragedy at this point on the trail.

Of this Bull Hunter was ignorant. He only knew that that angling rock would mask, from him who came second, whatever happened to the first rider. He could only pray that the first rider, as he surmised, would be Dunkin. If Pete Reeve came first it would be impossible to make the attack that he had planned. The terrible little gun fighter would be able to wheel in the saddle at the first alarm and end everything with one bullet.

Bull Hunter lay flat on his stomach at the cliff edge and looked down, waiting. The drop to the narrow trail—and how precariously narrow it seemed —was a full eighteen feet, and the rocky face to the crest was weatherworn to a glassy smoothness. So much he noted with satisfaction and then drew the rope up beside him and shook out the noose.

Below and beyond stretched a marvelous view of the bad lands, a chopped and broken country, still filled with pools of night. And over them the sky rose in a lovely arch, so near that it seemed to Bull he could stand up and touch the solid blue.

Day was coming fast, and it seemed to him that he could hear inarticulate noises of life awakening, though it was only the first faint morning breeze that was springing up. But now, down the trail, he heard unmistakable sounds of human voices, traveling toward him quickly. They seemed already on him and about to turn the curve, though the figure of The Ghost, slouching along the cliff, assured him that they were still a little distance off.

What they were saying he could not distinguish, for a thousand echoes confused the syllables. But now his attention was fixed on The Ghost, coming slowly closer to the elbow turn. The crisis was at hand. Who rode first, Reeve or Dunkin? Success or failure depended on the approaching figure.

And then he saw a horse's head, nodding as he came wearily around the turn, and then the level neck, and now the horn of the saddle! Dunkin rode into view!

Bull Hunter cast one swift glance upward, an involuntarily thanksgiving, then his grip settled more firmly on the rope. Dunkin raised his head. Bull's first emotion was to shrink back, but he remembered that a moving object quickly attracts attention. Dunkin was so far from expecting a human face above him that he probably would not see. And there he came, looking straight up, it seemed, into the eyes of Hunter. But apparently all he noticed was the blueness of the sky.

He dropped his head to curse a stumble of his horse, and at that instant Bull dropped the noose. There was one startled, "What the thunder," from Dunkin, as the circle dropped about his waist. Then Bull heaved up with all his strength, and the noose, sliding up under the strain, came taut and settled close, just under the arms of the victim. He was wrenched from the saddle at the first heave, and his yell of amazement and terror filled, it seemed to Bull Hunter, the whole width of the cañon.

An answering shout came, but Bull noted gratefully that it came from beyond the elbow turn. In the meantime he settled to his work. Hand over hand he whipped the screaming Dunkin up toward him. A frightened glance upward showed Dunkin that his persecutor stood above in the form of Hunter, and a fresh cry rose from his lips.

Soon the head of Pete Reeve's horse, nodding quickly from his trot, appeared in view, and then came Pete himself with poised gun. But his eyes were fastened down the trail at his own level; and as he glanced up with a shout of amazement at the spinning form of Dunkin, as the latter swung in mid-air, the victim was swung over the edge of the cliff. One fraction of an instant too late the bullet from Reeve's gun hummed over the head of the giant.

He gave no heed; neither did he hear the frantic cursing of the little man below, as he vainly strove to climb that glassy surface of the cliff. His attention was too much taken by the struggle with Dunkin.

It was very brief. In one mighty hand he gathered the wrists of the robber behind his back and tied them securely, and when the captive called afresh for help, Bull ground his face into the dirt. One dose of that treatment sufficed. Then Bull, carrying his trussed man over one arm, climbed into the saddle on Diablo. He rode the black close to the cliff.

"Pete!" he called. "Pete Reeve!"

The shouts of the little man, as he strove to climb the rock wall, ceased abruptly.

"Pete," said Bull, "I had to do it. You dunno how hard it was to go agin' you, but I had to do it. Will you forgive me?"

"Forgive you?" asked Pete Reeve. "No, curse

you, I'll never forgive you! You've sat with Dunkin around the fire. You've had chuck with him. And now you grab him for a reward!"

"You're wrong, Pete," answered the giant. "I swear I won't take a cent of the reward, not a cent. That isn't my reason."

"You lie," cried Reeve. "I've trusted you like a brother, and here's my reward. I've loved you like a son, but now I give you my word that I'll never stop off your trail, Bull, till I get you under my gun, and then one of us goes down for keeps!"

"I'll never fight you," said Bull solemnly, and he yearned to see the face of the little man below the rock.

"You coward!" retorted Reeve. "Then I'll tell the whole range you're yaller to the core!"

"It looks to me," said Bull mournfully, "like it's good-by. But I'll tell you this! Dunkin's no good. He never was any good; he's shot men from behind; he's robbed poor men; he's cheated with dice and cards. I've seen him when he cheated you, Pete, at your own camp fire. In spite of all that, I would never have touched him if it hadn't been that one person in the world asked me. And then I had to do it. Will you give me a chance and try to understand me? Old man, if you knew that——"

A harsh oath cut him short. "Stop whining," called Reeve. "If you're half a man, give Dunkin back to me, or show yourself and fight me for him. Will you do that?" His voice quivered with rage and entreaty.

"I can't."

"Then Heaven help one of us when we meet the next time!"

Bull hesitated. He loved this man who had been half father and half brother to him. "Pete," he said huskily, "will you listen to me say ten words?"

"If they're man-talk go ahead!"

"Pete, you can't keep up the life you're leading. They's no hope for it. You can beat the law nine times. The tenth time it'll beat you, and it only needs to beat you once to end you. Get out of this country and——"

"Say, shouted Pete Reeve, "are you sermonizing me?"

Bull Hunter turned the head of Diablo away and rode gloomily across the plateau, with Dunkin helpless on the saddle before him.

CHAPTER XX

A WOMAN'S WHIM

IN the town of White River they still tell how Bull Hunter brought Dunkin in. Fear, weariness and his uncomfortable position on the horse had made Dunkin wilt, and the celebrated robber and killer was a limp rag of a man when Bull Hunter literally handed him to the sheriff. The latter made preparations to secure the reward, put on the head of Dunkin, for Bull, but the giant refused absolutely to touch it.

"A lady asked me to bring him in," he said, "so I did it."

Then he turned joylessly on the trail to the Dunbar ranch. It was several days later when he reached it, and having had one bitter experience from blundering upon the house, he used some discretion on this occasion.

After all it was a surprisingly easy thing to do. He had only to wait in the shelter of the densest growth of trees until the men, to the very last one, had ridden out to their work of the day; then a little patience showed him Mary Hood walking in the garden. He waited until she was screened from the house by a hedge, and then he went out to her. He came rather diffidently, but the moment the girl saw him, she ran to him.

"Did you do it?" she asked eagerly. "How? When?"

She literally danced about him with impatience for his answer. Bull Hunter gazed at her in dismay and wonder and delight. Again she was dressed in white, all white from the soft hat on her head to her shoes. The wind kept a stir of silk about her, and her excitement made her smile and laugh and frown, all in a moment. It was only the third time that he had seen her, but she had apparently decided to let all barriers fall at once. Here, in a stride, he found himself admitted to her intimate friendship. Looking back to the long labor of the hunt for Dunkin, the capture, and even the parting with Pete Reeve, these were small things.

"Yes," he was able to answer her at last. "I did it."

"But how? I want to know every bit of it."

Bull Hunter raised his face into the wind, as though hoping that it might bring him inspiration. "There isn't much to it," he said. "I just got on his trail, warned him I was coming and what I was going to try to do, and then I happened to catch him and bring him into the town of White River."

"And that's all there is to it?" asked the girl, smiling faintly.

"That's all."

She broke out at him, laughing: "But I know the whole story, Charlie. I know how you followed him and caught him in a noose, with that terrible Pete Reeve not far away; and I know how you rode into White River; and I know you refused the reward. It was a fine thing to do; it was a brave thing to do, Charlie, and the whole range is talking about it!"

She stopped, a little afraid that her enthusiasm had made her go too far, but one glance at his flushed, embarrassed face reassured her. "But you are not rich, and yet you refused a two-thousand-dollar reward. Why did you do that? The money is yours."

"Of course I couldn't take it," answered Bull Hunter. "I'd already been paid for the job."

"Paid for it?"

"Yes."

He raised a hand to his throat and presently lifted above the edge of his shirt a thin chain of gold; and she knew that that was how he kept her locket. In spite of herself, she flushed. There were so many qualities of modesty, gallantry, pride and simplicity about this giant of a man that he continually took her by surprise.

"That's a pleasant thing to say to me," she answered softly. "Thank you."

"Besides," continued Bull, who had not quite finished with his thought, "if there is any reward coming it would have to come from you."

She regarded him with something of a smile. Perhaps he was not quite so simple as she had suspected. "In what way?" she asked him.

"In a lot of ways," said Bull. "But first I'd like to know why you were so anxious to catch him."

"Because he had taken that locket, of course," she replied.

"No; I was bringing you the locket when you asked me to go for him; and you gave me the locket for taking him."

She was stopped completely. "I don't like examinations," she told him with a frown. "To tell you the truth I didn't really care a whit about it. But you seemed so eager to do something for me, and that thing happened to pop into my mind."

"You didn't have a real reason for wanting to have him caught?" asked Bull Hunter in amazement.

"You looked so big and so young and so strong that day," she explained, "that just for a moment I felt as if I were the lady and you were the knight out of some old story book. So I sent you to capture the villain, and the only villain I could think of, you see, was this Dunkin, the robber. My father is almost willing to forgive you for the old quarrel, because you took Dunkin in such a clever way."

She stopped; the face of Bull Hunter was very grave.

"It sort of drifts in on me, little by little," he said slowly. "You didn't have no real reason for wanting Dunkin taken. It just popped into your mind?"

He walked up and down, and the girl, looking at the huge strides, the head bent in thought and the heavily puckered forehead, lost a little of her elation.

Presently he stopped before her again. He had been worshiping her beauty every moment of their talk, but now she saw a shadow in his eyes and she was alarmed. It was not, she told herself at once, that she cared particularly for this big, dull-witted fellow, but—she found it impossible to define what she did feel. With the solemn eyes of the big man resting upon her, she had a positive reaction of guilt.

"Mary Hood," he said at length, "that was a long trail and a hard one. There was three men that might have died, instead of just one being captured unhurt, till the law hurts him. I didn't know why you wanted him taken. I didn't ask. Just that you wanted it was enough for me; and it still is. I'll forget what's happened; I'll forget that Dunkin is in jail and due to hang——"

"But he's not in jail," broke in the girl. "Surely you heard what happened?"

"Eh?" asked Bull Hunter.

"Of course he's not in jail. He wasn't in White River a single night. You see, that terrible little man, Pete Reeve, rode down out of the mountains and in the middle of the night attacked the jail; he shot down two of the guards and left them badly wounded, then he set Dunkin free."

Bull Hunter closed his eyes, smiling faintly. He could see that picture, the little active gun fighter in his glory, storming the jail, the spit and bark of the guns, the crunching of bullets against the old brick walls. "And then they rode away together?" asked Bull Hunter.

"Dunkin rode away, but not Pete Reeve."

"What!"

He came close to her, grown terrible all at once; and he stretched out his hands for the explanation, as though he were stretching them out to seize and crush her. She had never before been able to understand, in spite of his bulk, how this mild-voiced fellow could ever be formidable to fighting men. But a full realization of what he might be in action came suddenly to her and dazed her.

"Not Pete Reeve?" asked Bull Hunter, still following her, as she shrank away.

"Does he mean as much to you as all that?"

"As much as that? As much as the world! He's saved my life and made me a man and taught me everything I know and been my friend. What's happened to him?"

"It happened in the jail—I don't know. It just came to me by hearsay, and there's nothing definite."

He turned gray with fear and suddenly caught her hands. "They killed Pete Reeve?" he asked. Then his voice thundered: "They killed Pete Reeve! And I'll break a dozen of 'em to bits for it. They killed him! Pete Reeve is dead!"

"No, no! I give you my word. What I heard was that a bullet grazed his head and then knocked him unconscious——"

"But Dunkin stayed over the body like a brave man," said Bull in his agony. "Dunkin stayed there and fought them off. He stayed till Pete Reeve got his senses back, and then they fought their way through and got clear. Tell me, was that what happened?"

He still held her hands, and his face showed a dozen emotions. The girl shrank from him in her distress. There was as much difference between the placid Bull Hunter, whom she had known before, and this raging giant, as the difference between a June sky and a thunderstorm.

"I wish I could say it. That was what you would have done, I know. You'd have stayed and fought them off for your friend. But Dunkin, whom Pete Reeve had just saved, when he saw his friend drop, simply turned and ran for his life and rode away on Reeve's horse!"

The chin of Bull Hunter dropped on his breast, and his hands fell limply away from hers.

"But is it so terrible? Won't he be able——"

"He'll hang," said Bull Hunter simply. "He's killed ten men, all in fair fight, and not a one of 'em but deserved the killing. But his record is long and black. This is the end of Pete Reeve." He lifted his head. "Unless I could do something!" he whispered. "Oh, if I could do something!"

She caught a dizzy glimpse into the future; she saw the giant, plunging on the guards at the jail in White River. "But they've changed everything. Since Dunkin got away they have half a dozen men sleeping in the front room of the jail. You won't do some mad thing?"

"Mary," he said, "Pete Reeve has been my partner."

There was no answer to this. All her arguments dried up in her throat and left her staring blankly at him. She felt, as she had never felt before, the mighty power of the friendship between man and man. It made the people she had grown up with seem paltry creatures. What would her father do for a friend in need? What would Hal Dunbar himself, for all his might of hand, do in the service of a man whose life was threatened by the law? But here was one who would risk his own life.

A panic took her, and yet she was thrilling with happiness at the thought of him. When her eyes cleared she saw that he was holding out his hand, and when she extended hers to meet it, she felt the locket and gold chain drop into her palm, still warm from the body of the giant.

She stared at him without understanding.

"I'll never see you again," said Bull Hunter. "Maybe I'll get bumped off when I try to bust the jail; maybe not. But my trail will never come back here. Now that I'm going I'll talk frank to you. I've loved you, Mary; I've worshiped you; I've kept you in front of me night and day. The thought of you kept me honest when I was living with thieves, and just a wish that you wouldn't explain, made me go out and risk three men's lives and lose my friend. I didn't care. A touch of your hand was worth more to me than all that. But now, just for a whim of yours, Pete Reeve is dead—worse than dead, because, all the days he's in there at that jail, he's bound to think of what's coming to him. And he was meant for a death under an open sky. He was meant for a fighting death that other men would never forget. Because of you he's trapped.

"And I see you for the first time. There's no thought in you except for yourself. There's no generosity in your nature. You never think of giving, but always of taking."

She tried to go back from him; she wanted desperately to turn and flee to the house, but the steady, sad voice still held her.

"You've taught me one thing that may be worth all the rest. They ain't a thing in the world after this that I can trust because of what it seems to be. Not a thing! I'll forget what trusting people means. And the worst of it is, I know, that I'll keep on loving you, Mary Hood, to the end of my life."

Then he was gone. She saw him swing across the garden and disappear among the trees; presently she heard the rush of a galloping horse through the underbrush.

The locket slipped from her hand, struck the catch in its fall and lay open at her feet. Mary Hood stamped on the lovely face of the miniature and turned and fled to the house.

CHAPTER XXI

THE CHOICE

THERE was cruel work for Diablo on that back trail to the town of White River, for Bull Hunter rode like a madman, hardly stopping for food and sleep. When they reached the little village Bull went straight to the jail.

The moment he set foot in the street it was apparent that the town considered him a distinguished visitor. He saw women in gingham come to doors and stand with their arms akimbo, smiling and nodding at him. A boy ran fearlessly out and strove to shake hands with him as he swept by. A little crowd gathered in his wake, like dust behind a wind, and followed him to the jail.

When he went through the door he was accorded a real reception. The "half dozen" guards, of whom Mary had spoken, proved to be only three, but they sat in the front room of the jail, armed to the teeth with rifle, revolver, and even prominently displayed knives. Plainly the next visitor who came unannounced to the White River jail, would be accorded a reception which he would never forget.

The sheriff introduced Bull to the guards, and they shook hands with the carelessness of Westerners who wish to prove that they are not overimpressed on meeting a distinguished man. But Bull Hunter was too unhappy to notice. The sheriff immediately afterward drew him into his little office.

"I've news for you, Hunter," he said, "and great news at that. You surprised me a good deal when you wouldn't take that two thousand on the head of Dunkin. A good thing for you that you didn't, because Dunkin would have been gone before you got the money. But there's better game than that for you, Hunter, a lot better."

He settled back in his chair and smiled benevolently upon the giant. "Matter of fact we want men like you around White River. If I had a fellow like you to call on as a deputy now and then, when a hard job comes up, there'd be such a falling off in crime around these parts that it'd make your head swim. Yes, sir! And now, Hunter, I've been in touch with the authorities to find out if there's any need of paying the reward on the head of Pete Reeve. The man whose bullet stunned him won't get it—wouldn't take it if he could, because he happens to be the richest man in these parts. But we all figure it out that, if you hadn't taken Dunkin, Reeve would never have come in and practically put himself in our hands, so to speak. That reward needs a taker, and with a little work on the side, I think I could get it for you. In return for that——"

"Sheriff," broke in Bull Hunter, "it's kind of you to think of all this, but I don't want the reward."

The sheriff gaped.

"You see," said Bull Hunter, "I've just come in to look things over, to see if Reeve was really here. That's all."

They were interrupted by the sound of a blast behind the building.

"Chopping out a foundation for a new jail," explained the sheriff. "Want to see it?"

Bull assented, and as they went out and around the building, the sheriff went on: "This old jail of ours is a pretty rickety affair. One of these days them brick walls'll tumble down. We'd been figuring on putting up a new one for some time, and that little jail-busting stunt of Reeve's woke us up. Boys been hard at the foundations ever since. We're going to have a cellar, as you see. Main trouble is that they hit rock, right under the surface, and they're having to bite it out with powder. Hello, there's a whopper!"

They had come around to the rear of the jail by this time, and they saw two men struggling out with a ponderous, jagged rock which had been torn loose by the last explosion. Other rocks in piles and heaps of dirt had been taken from a small rectangular excavation.

"The new walls are going to be stone," said the sheriff, "and then we'll have something that'll keep us safe and sound. Until that time," he went on, as they turned back, "we need good deputies handy. Wonder if you'd think about settling down here? Of course you don't mean what you said about refusing the reward. Why, man, add up all that's offered by some and sundry, and it comes to round about ten thousand!"

"I'll think it over," said Bull. "Meantime I'd like to see Reeve if I may."

The sheriff was perfectly cordial. He took Bull to the outer room and pointed to a door. "That leads to the jail room. Nobody but Reeve in it. He's got no weapons, of course. Think you could trust yourself in there alone with him?"

It was exactly what Bull wanted. He smiled, and

the sheriff unlocked the door and waved Bull inside.

It was a low, square room, so dark that he could barely make out Pete Reeve, smoking unconcernedly at the far end of it. The sheriff closed the door, and they were alone. But Pete Reeve, eying the visitor from head to foot, seemed to be quite unaware of his presence.

Bull crossed the room to him and stood above the cot where the little man sat. He seemed smaller than ever; his hair was grayer; now that the law had him in its grip he seemed to have aged ten years. Put him out in the open on a strong horse, and he would soon recover his vigor. But now Bull Hunter looked down on him with pity and a touch of horror.

"I don't expect you to talk to me, Pete," he said gently. "If you had a gun with you, I know the sort of talk you'd make. You haven't, and I don't blame you much for not speaking. But the point is that Dunkin has shown himself the same sort of skunk that I told you he was. You thought he was worth fighting for; but he wasn't. He run off and left you cold in the lurch, Pete. That's his kind.

"I've come to tell you that I'm going to get you out, or do something that'll put me in here with you."

There was one spark of light in the eyes of the little man; it went out almost at once. Then he said slowly: "And how are you going to break in?"

"Through that wall," answered Bull instantly. He pointed to the back wall of the jail. "That door into the outside room opens back. Can you wedge it to-night, so's it can't be opened easy, in case the guards try to run in?"

Pete Reeve stood up suddenly and gripped the arm

of the giant. "Why, boy," he answered, "I think you mean business. But what about the wall? You don't mean to come through a big brick wall?"

"I probably won't be able to," said Bull Hunter, "but I'm going to try. You do your part about the door."

"One thing else," said Pete Reeve. "Have you got a gun on you besides the one in your holster?"

"I always have," said Bull. "You taught me that, Pete."

The little man rubbed his hands in an ecstasy. "Good boy! Give me that extra gun and I'll do my own share about getting myself out."

Bull shook his head. "When we make the break to-night we're going to get away without shooting a gun, or else let ourselves drop without firing back. Is that straight to you, Pete?"

"It's crazy, that's what it is. No sense to it. Whoever heard of breaking jail without a gun play?"

"We'll make history, then," replied Bull Hunter. "What I say goes to-night."

"Not in a thousand years."

"Are you going to stay and wait for the rope? Rather do that than die full of good, honest lead?"

"Stop, Bull," said Reeve. "The hangman's knot is tied under my ear every night in my dreams. You win, Bull. What you say goes for to-night."

Bull shook hands with him silently, and they parted.

CHAPTER XXII

THE TWO VERSIONS

THERE were two versions of what happened that night in White River, that most historic of all nights in the town. The one is the version of Mrs. Caswell; and the other is the version of the sheriff.

Mrs. Caswell lived in the little house opposite the rear of the jail. As she told the story, the night was so very warm that she could not sleep. Moreover, being an old woman of sixty-five, her sleep at all times was easily disturbed.

She tossed in her bed for a long time and finally got up and put on a dress and went to sit on her little veranda and watch the stars. Because, as she said, stars are "tolerable quieting when you pick 'em out, one by one, and look hard."

This night, however, the stars were dimmed by the whitest of white moonlight. So brilliant was the moon indeed, that it dazzled the eyes of Mrs. Caswell, and she looked down to the earth instead.

And so it happened that she saw a giant out of a fairy tale walk slowly up to the rear of the jail. He was so huge, even at that distance, that she adjusted her glasses and stared again to make sure.

This huge man, having come to the rear of the jail, looked about him for a moment, as though searching for something on the ground. At length he seemed to have found what he wanted. He stooped and rose again, bearing a large object in his hands. With this he approached the rear wall of the jail. There she saw him brace his legs far apart and then swing the object, which was of great size, above his head.

Once, twice, and again he struck the wall of the jail, and the dull sound of the blows came to her distinctly. Following the last there was a rush and a roar and a ragged section of the wall collapsed, exposing the dark interior. Out of this darkness a small figure darted, small as a child beside the giant, and the two raced across the open.

At the same time a great hubbub broke out from the front of the jail, and presently other men plunged through the dark gap in the rear wall and ran after the two fugitives, firing shots. The latter, however, came to two horses near some cottonwoods, swung into the saddle and were at once gone at a racing pace; after which Mrs. Caswell, her ears full of the sound of shots and yells, and her mind full of giants and elves, collapsed.

The sheriff's narrative was even simpler.

He sat among the three guards of the night shift waiting for the morrow, when his distinguished and formidable prisoner should be taken from his hands and carried to a safer prison. It was well after midnight. Every one was fagged, and they drank coffee steadily to keep on the alert.

Without warning they heard a blow at the rear of the jail and felt a shock that shook the floor beneath them.

They remained motionless, stunned with surprise. Some one said that it must be a blast from the excavation at the rear. The words were not out of his mouth when the blow and shock were repeated. The sheriff then sprang up and tried the door, but it failed to give under his hand and seemed to be securely wedged on the inside. At the same time there was another blow, this time accompanied by a great crashing and rending sound of falling brick, and the voice of Pete Reeve calling: "Good boy! That does it!"

The sheriff shouted. Two of his guards lunged at the door and knocked it open. When they reached the hole in the rear wall, the fugitives were far away in the moonlight and could not be brought down. There was a hot chase, but a useless one.

They returned and examined the scene of the break, using lanterns. Here they found what the sheriff was certain was the implement used in breaking down the wall. It was a gigantic stone, with the face of it battered from the pounding against the bricks. Two of the sheriff's men essayed to lift it and succeeded only with the greatest difficulty. Accordingly they agreed that it would be impossible for any one man to use such a massive object as a tool to be swung in the hands.

But every one agreed that, if there were a man in the world capable of swinging that mass of rock above his head, it must be Bull Hunter and no other. These details answered Mrs. Caswell's description of the giant, and the sheriff had a warrant for the apprehension of Bull Hunter sworn out in due legal form, and a reward for his arrest was immediately added.

It may be noted that the rock which Bull Hunter used as a hammer is now on exhibition in the new White River jail.

CHAPTER XXIII

A DECISION

"SOMETHING has to be done," said big Hal Dunbar, and his handsome face clouded as he spoke.

His ranch foreman, listening, swallowed a groan. For nearly fifteen years he had worked the will of this heir to the great Dunbar ranch and watched the headstrong child grow into the imperious, tyrannical man, sullen and dangerous whenever his will was thwarted. But closely as Jack Hood knew his young master, he had never seen Dunbar half so gloomy as to-day.

In his hand, as he spoke, Dunbar held out a small trinket, consisting of a gold chain, broken in several places, and what seemed to be a crushed and disfigured locket.

"You understand?" he repeated, as he dropped the locket into the hand of Jack Hood.

The latter examined it and saw the miniature photograph of a woman's face, but hopelessly marred, scratched, and crushed beyond recognition of the features.

"Good heavens!" he muttered presently. "It's Mary's locket. She'll be a wild one when she finds out this has happened." Then he started as another idea came into his mind. "But where, Hal—how did you get this? Or am I going crazy? Wasn't this stole from me by that skunk, Dunkin, and ain't he half a hundred miles away, and——"

Hal Dunbar interrupted calmly enough: "Wait a minute. I'll tell you a few things that link up with all this. You remember it was a month ago yesterday that I asked Mary for the hundredth time to marry me?"

"Guess it was about then."

"It was exactly then," reiterated Dunbar. "That was the time she said she would marry me in six weeks to the day."

"Yes, I remember."

"Then, the next morning, that blundering fool, Bull Hunter, appeared, and we chased him."

"Chased him out of sight. I nearly rode the blue roan to death that day." The foreman grinned at the memory.

"But we didn't ride far enough for all that," said Dunbar growlingly. "The hound must have doubled back on us."

"Eh?"

The patience of Hal Dunbar left him. Suddenly his face was suffused an ugly red. He was thundering the words: "I tell you he must have doubled back, and he saw your daughter while the rest of us were riding our horses to death on a blind trail. That's what happened, and this is how I know. When I got back, Mary was in her room and said she had a headache. When she did come down she wouldn't say a word about the marriage, and a little while later she said that she couldn't think of marrying me inside of six weeks. She wanted longer. She wouldn't give me any definite answer at all."

"I remember," said Jack Hood, nodding.

"You remember? Then why the devil don't you do something about it? You let your girl treat me as if she was the lady of the land and I a slave, or something." He controlled himself a little and went on: "Well, it never came into my head why she had changed her mind so quick that day, till this morning I was out walking in the garden, and I come on this, behind a bush. You know what it is?"

"Yep. It's Mary's locket. Plumb spoiled."

"Do you know who spoiled it?"

"I dunno. Some idiot."

"She did it herself!"

"What!"

"I saw a print over it. That happened pretty near a month ago, but it was stamped into the ground where the garden mold was soft, and where it hasn't been disturbed since. So there was a shadow of a print of the foot left, and the print was Mary's shoe."

"Can't be," said Jack Hood, shaking his head.

"Who else around here has a foot no bigger'n a child's?"

Jack Hood was silenced.

"I can tell you just about what happened," continued Hal Dunbar. "Bull Hunter came here to see Mary. He blundered up in full view, and we chased him. He dodged away from us and circled back to the house. When he arrived he found Mary alone in the garden, and he came up and talked to her. What he returned for was to give back that locket. But they talked about other things, too, and in the end Mary was so cut up that she stamped the locket he had brought her into the ground."

Jack Hood sat as one stunned. "I dunno," he repeated again. "I don't understand!"

"Sure, you don't," said Hal Dunbar with a snarl.

"Sure, you don't understand what they could of talked about. But one thing is sure—they weren't talking about the price of beef on foot! Why has Mary been glum this whole month? Why has she had a frown for me every time I came near her? I tell you that Bull Hunter has some sort of a hold on her, Heaven knows how!"

Her father shook his head. "Then how come she'd leave the locket lying there a whole month, pretty near?"

"Just another proof that she was all wrought up that day. She was so excited she was blind. She dropped the locket and stamped on it and then ran away. When her senses came back to her, she goes to the garden to look for it again, but she's forgotten just where she left it, and, besides, maybe a little dust had blown over it and kept it from shining. It was kind of under a bush, too. That explains it easy enough. And sometimes I think, Hood, that your girl is in love with that murdering outlaw!"

The attack on his daughter's taste roused Hood to momentary remonstrance.

"He ain't a murderer!"

"Didn't he shoot you down?"

"Because I got mad about nothing and picked a fight with him and got what was coming to me. He could of killed me that day—he only winged me instead."

"Well, let the murder side of it go. At least you have to admit that he's an outlaw?"

"And what for?" exclaimed Jack Hood with heat. "Because a friend of his that happened to be a robber got stuck in jail? And because Bull Hunter went down to White River like a man and got Pete Reeve out of the jail? They talk about how he done it still. Sure they outlawed him for doing it, but I'd like to have one or two friends that would break the law because they was that fond of me!"

"I see how it is," said Dunbar bitterly. "You agree with Mary. You want her to marry him. Well, go ahead and take her to him. Go ahead. I won't stop you."

"Listen," replied Jack Hood. "D'you think I'm a fool? I'd rather see her dead, pretty near, than thrown away on Hunter."

"Yep," said Hal Dunbar, nodding, "you show some sense. You want Mary to own the ranch one of these days, and so do I. She's the one for the place. She's the lady to do it. But"—and here he began to beat out his points by striking his fist into the palm of his other hand—"she'll never marry me while Bull Hunter is alive. Hood, for your sake and my sake and, in the long run, for Mary's sake, too, that fellow has got to die!"

Jack Hood wiped his perspiring forehead.

"Talk softer, Hal," he said pleadingly. "You don't mean what you just said, and if you do mean it, it's just because you're wrought up over finding this here locket, and——"

"Send for Mary, and I'll prove I'm right."

"How? By asking her questions?"

"I'm not a fool. I don't pretend to be as clever as she is. That's one reason I want to marry her— because I'm proud of her, Jack."

The foreman smiled and nodded. He had no real affection for Hal Dunbar, but he had a deep and abiding love for the Dunbar ranch which he had run for so many years, and the bright dream of his life was to see Mary Hood the mistress of those wide lands.

"If it comes to the pinch, Hal," he said, "I can make Mary marry you, and I'll do it. She's learned one thing—and that's to obey me. I'm not a soft man. I've taught my girl to do what I tell her to do, and if it comes to the pinch, I'll order her to marry you. Ain't it the best for her? Could she ever do better? No, sir! She couldn't!"

"Maybe she couldn't," said Hal Dunbar, greatly mollified. "And—you go as far as you like about persuading her, Jack. I've tried my hand long enough. Here it is three years since I first started to get Mary to marry me, and now I'm further away from it than ever. But I aim to find out where I stand. Will you call her in here?"

Jack Hood looked at him earnestly for a moment and then went to the door. "Mary!" he called.

His voice rang through the hall, and finally the answer came, thin, and small, from a distance, swelling suddenly out at them as a door was opened.

"Coming, dad."

They could hear her feet tapping swiftly down the stairs.

At the door she paused before she came in and smiled at them, very beautiful with her dark hair and her dark eyes. Hal Dunbar lowered his own glance quickly.

"Jim Laurel just come over from White River way," he said carelessly, "and Jim gave us some news that might interest you. You remember the name of the gent that stole your locket from Jack?"

"Dunkin was the name, wasn't it?"

"That was it. You got a mighty good memory, Mary. Well, Jim says that Dunkin's been caught."

"Oh," said the girl, "and did they get my locket from him?"

Hal Dunbar looked up at her in open admiration. For a moment his own conviction that she knew all about the locket was shaken, but he went on.

"No; didn't hear Jim speak about any locket. But it's quite a story—that yarn about the taking of Dunkin. There was another fellow with him, an outlaw, of course. They got cornered. The other gent was filled full of lead, and Dunkin surrendered."

"Who was the other man?" she asked without too much interest, for many such tales had she heard, and this was by no means violent compared with some.

"The other man?" said Dunbar, apparently trying to remember, but in reality watching her like a hawk. "His name," he finally drawled, "is Bull Hunter!"

Dunbar had expected some slight paling, some infinitesimal start, for Mary was always well poised; but the result of his bluff was astonishing. Every sinew in her body seemed to be suddenly unstrung. She dropped into the chair behind her and sat watching them with a deadly white face and numb lips that kept repeating the name of Bull Hunter soundlessly. There could have been no greater proof than that sudden change of expression. She loved Bull Hunter! Her father bowed his head. Hal Dunbar stared at her as one who has lost his last hope in life.

"It was a joke, Mary," he said gloomily. "It was just a trick to find out where you stood, and it worked a lot better than I expected—or a lot worse!"

The color struck back into her face in a wonderful manner.

"Are you telling true, Hal?" she cried. "They—they didn't kill him?"

He shook his head, sick at heart.

"Thank God!" cried Mary Hood.

And then she realized how completely she had betrayed herself. She saw it in the bowed head of her father and the drawn face of Hal Dunbar. She rose to escape, but at the door she turned and faced them.

"It was a cowardly thing to do," she said. "It was a base, base thing to do. But I thank you for it, Hal. Do you know that I've been in doubt of how I really felt about him? But now you've helped me to know the truth. I love him. I'm proud of it!"

CHAPTER XXIV

IMPRISONED

FOR a long moment after she left, the two men struggled to recover from the shock, and then Jack Hood rose and began to pace the room.

"I don't believe it," he said. "I can't believe it. Think of throwing her away on an outlaw and——"

"You were defending him a minute ago," said Dunbar bitterly.

"Curse him!" said Jack Hood with emphasis. "To sneak in here and take her away from you like a thief—why, he hasn't seen her more than three times!"

Hal Dunbar writhed as much in shame as in anger, crying: "What did he do? How did he talk to her? That great, stupid, block of a man! A child has more sense!"

"It's what is called an infatuation," decided Jack Hood. "I'm going up to try to talk her into her right senses. If I can't do that——"

"Well?"

"I'll take her away, to begin with. There are ways of teaching girls obedience. I'll find one that will work!"

"What would you do?"

"Leave that to me. I guess you want me to go far enough?"

"As far as you like," said Dunbar miserably.

Jack Hood grasped his hand and then hurried from the room with the will to do or die.

Straight to the door of Mary's chamber he went and found it locked. In return for his noisy rapping she finally opened it a fraction of an inch.

"What——" she began, but he violently pushed the door open the rest of the way and entered.

It was his way of asserting his mastery.

When he came in, however, he received another shock. His daughter's face was flushed, and tears were on her cheeks.

He interpreted this to suit himself, manlike.

"I'm glad to see you've got your senses back," he said. "You made a fool of yourself down there. But it ain't so bad that you can't make up for it. Hal still wants you—Heaven knows why, after the way you've acted!"

"But I don't want him," she answered disdainfully. "I detest him."

"Eh?" sputtered her father, amazed.

"Suppose it had been true?" she gasped out. "Suppose they had really cornered Charlie Hunter? He'd fight to the last drop of blood in him. Oh, don't I know the sort of a man he is? But suppose it were true? How do I know what's happening to him? Dad, we've got to get him away from——"

"Look here!" interrupted her father angrily. "D'you mean to tell me that you been up here crying like a baby because of what might happen to Bull Hunter?"

He shook her arm, but there was no resistance. The spitfire he had known as his daughter was gone, and in her place stood a misty-eyed girl he hardly recognized. Some strange thing had happened to change her, and the grim old fellow very shrewdly guessed that it was love indeed. It abashed him and puzzled him. Also, it profoundly enraged him.

"You've played the idiot once too often," he said sternly. "Hal knows about everything. He has the locket that Bull Hunter brought back to you and——"

"Do you know what he did?" said the girl with a sudden transport of enthusiasm. "He took that locket and brought it to me. But he wanted it for himself. I was like a foolish girl. He talked like a knight of the old days. I wanted to try him out. So I told him he could keep the locket if he would capture Dunkin and turn him over to the law. And he did it!" She laughed with excitement at the thought. "He captured Dunkin alive and brought him to a jail. Then one of his friends, Pete Reeve, tried to rescue Dunkin and did it—but got caught himself. Charlie Hunter didn't know of it until he came back here to tell me he had captured Dunkin as I asked him to do. But when I told him what had happened he turned on me and told me he scorned me. He talked to me as no man ever talked to me. He showed me how wickedly vain and foolish I had been. Three men were in peril of their lives because I had asked him to do a thing in which I had no real interest, nothing but a whim. When he knew Pete Reeve was in jail he swore he would get him out or die in the effort. And that's how he left me. He'll never see me again, dad. But he did what he said he would do. He went down to the jail—he smashed the wall of it—he took his friend away and was outlawed for it."

She threw out her hands in a gesture of what was both appeal and triumph.

"And when I know a man like that, how can you ask me to love such a fellow as Hal Dunbar?"

Her father bit his lip. It was even worse than he had dared to suspect.

"Love is one thing and marriage is another," he said. "You got your children to think about when you marry. How could you take care of children if you married a wild man like Hunter?"

"If I love him, everything else will take care of itself."

"Bosh!" roared Jack Hood.

She shrugged her shoulders.

"I've reasoned enough with you," said her father. "Now comes the time to tell you what you'll do. You'll marry Hal Dunbar, girl, if I have to drag you to it."

She looked at him with a sort of fierce contempt that changed slowly to wonder and then to fear.

"Do you think for a minute, dad, that even if you would do such a horrible thing, Hal Dunbar would accept such a marriage? Hasn't he the pride of his family?"

"He's got pride enough, but he's in love—bad. And he'll do anything to get you. Understand? Look here, Mary. I'm fond of you, but I'm fond of the work I've given my life to. That work has been to make you the lady of the Dunbar ranch, and you're going to be that whether you want to or not. Is that clear?"

"Perfectly," she said faintly. "But you don't understand, dad. There aren't such things as forced marriages these days."

"Aren't there?" he said sneeringly, red with his anger. He went to the door. "I'm not asking you for any promises, Mary. Treat me square, and I'll be the easiest father you ever seen. Cross me, and I'll raise more rumpus in a minute than you ever seen in a year. Understand? Now think this over till morning. That's plenty of time. Take every angle of it and give it a look. It's worth taking your time about."

And so he was gone.

It was a very unnecessary touch, but he could not resist it. As he closed the door behind him, he turned the key in the lock and removed it.

But the moment she heard the sound, the lips of Mary Hood curled. She had been badly frightened before; she was badly frightened now, remembering many brutal ways in which he had treated her mother; but when she heard that turning of the lock which proclaimed her a forced prisoner, she revolted. It was just a little too much.

She went, naturally, to the window. To climb down would be the simplest thing in the world. There was a drop of ten feet to the ground from the first row of windows, but that would be nothing to her. The main problem was where would she go once she was on the ground? Easy enough to get there, but where flee once she had escaped?

The influence of Hal Dunbar spread over the mountains very, very far, and every soul in the ranges knew that she was expected to become the wife of the rich rancher. No matter in which direction she rode, she would be quickly taken at the first house where she stopped for food or shelter and returned to the ranch.

Still she could not believe that the whole affair was more than a hoax to break her spirit. She refused to take anything seriously until evening, when there was a tap at the door to warn her, and then the rattle of a key in the lock. Presently, without requesting permission to enter, the door swung open and the old Chinese cook appeared.

Now, the ancient Chinaman had been the pet and the object of the girl's teasing all her life, and her face brightened when she saw him. But the old fellow placed a tray of food—at least they were not going to try to starve her—on a chair and backed out the door, keeping an immobile expression. She went after him, calling out in anger, but he stepped quickly into the hall, and the door closed in her face.

The grating of the lock had a new meaning to her now. It declared very definitely that her father had meant what he said. They were going to try force. And if the old Chinaman whom she had teased and petted all her life could be turned against her so easily, what trust could she put in any man on the ranch?

There was only one place she could go, and that was to Charlie Hunter, big and fearless and trustworthy to the end, she knew. Somewhere in the northern mountains he lurked. How she could find a way to him when the posse which was hunting for Bull Hunter and Pete Reeve had failed, was another mystery, but the attempt must be made. Otherwise —there was the marriage with Hal Dunbar. She had looked forward to it all her life without repulsion, but now that it was inevitable it became a horror.

CHAPTER XXV

FLIGHT

THE long hours wore away, and the noises of life in the house were at last hushed. She waited still longer, hooding her lamp so that not a ray of light could reach either the window or the door. Then she began her preparations.

They were comparatively simple. She put on a riding skirt and packed some changes of clothes in a small bundle. Then she strapped the light .32 revolver with its cartridge belt around her waist and put the big, flaring sombrero on her head. She caught a glimpse of herself in the half-darkened mirror, and the sight of the slender body and the pale face with wide, frightened eyes, disturbed her. She was surely a small force to be pitted against the brain of Jack Hood and the power of Hal Dunbar!

Yet she went on, with only the terror now that some one might come before she was out of the room.

She opened the window with infinite pains lest there should be a squeak of wood against wood, or a rattle of the sash. But there was no sound, and now she leaned out the window.

What had seemed so simple during the daylight now became a desperate thing indeed. The dark ground seemed a perilous distance below her, and what if her foot should slip as she climbed down toward the sill of the first window from which she was to drop? She slipped one leg over the sill and listened again.

The wind was full of whispers like light laughter. Yet she went on, though fear made the grip of her hands weak and kept her foot slipping from its hold as she climbed. She reached the broad molding above the window of the first story. She dropped perilously toward the lower sill and then lost her balance and toppled back.

The scream that jumped into her throat swelled to aching, yet she kept it back. It was a short fall, but to the girl, as she shot through the air, it seemed that death must come at the end of it. Then her feet struck deep in the garden mold, and she toppled on her back. She lay a minute with the breath knocked out of her, slowly gasping to recover, and then picked herself up with care.

She was unhurt, a little muddy from the newly wetted garden soil, but otherwise as sound as when she began the descent. She now turned straight across the garden to the barn. There the mare, Nancy, whinnied a greeting and rubbed a soft muzzle against her cheek. The girl cast her arms around the neck of the horse and hugged the familiar head close to her. Here, at least, was one true friend in a world of enemies!

The saddling was a slow process, for every now and then she had to stop to listen to the noises in the barn, little creaking sounds as the horses stirred on the wooden floor, and very like the noise of men approaching stealthily to seize her.

At last the saddle was on, and she led Nancy out the back door of the barn, let down the bars, and stepped onto the muffling grass of the field beyond;

then into the saddle, trembling when the leather stirrup creaked under her weight in mounting; then down the hollow, fearful lest one of the horses in the neighboring corrals might neigh and bring an answer from Nancy.

But there was not a sound. Now, looking back, the house on the hill was huge and black, and Mary Hood wondered how she could ever have been happy in it, but she had hardly drawn one great breath of relief when the deep night of the trees closed over her. She had ridden through those trees a hundred times before at night, but always in company with others, and now they were changed and strange, and the solemn, small noises of the night were before and behind her.

The little bay mare went daintily and wisely. She knew every nook and cranny of that wood. Every stump and tree and every root that worked up out of the ground was familiar. Once or twice a twig snapped under her foot, but on the whole she kept to the noiseless ground.

Mary Hood let the horse go as she would. Her way led north. That she knew and little else, for she had heard a rumor that Pete Reeve and Bull Hunter were in the Tompson Mountains. And since the mare had chosen that way by instinct it began to seem that her ride was fated to succeed. Moreover, the wind of the galloping exhilarated her, and the darkness was no longer complete. Instead, the stars burned closer and closer to her through the thin mountain air.

To reach the Tompsons required a two days' journey, and she remembered now with a start that she had taken no provisions with her. Neither had she more than touched her supper that night. She gathered the reins to turn back, but at this moment Nancy shied from a white stone and doubled her speed straight north. All people in danger are superstitious, and Mary Hood took that little incident, coming when it did, as a sign from Heaven that she must not double back.

The stars were beginning to fade when she reached the first foothills, and by sunrise she was among the upper peaks, desperately hungry and with an ache at the base of her brain from lack of sleep. Nancy, too, was very tired. She plodded willingly on, but her head was neither so proud nor so high. She had ceased thinking for herself, and like every tired horse was surrendering her destiny into the hands of the rider.

At the first small stream they reached, a tiny trickle of spring water, the girl dismounted and bathed her face and throat and let Nancy drink a little and nibble some of the grass near the water. Then she went on again, greatly refreshed. Her sleepiness grew less now that the sun was bright, and with that brightness her chances of success seemed far greater.

But before very long she knew she was coming into a district crossed by many riders, and it would be far wiser for her to lie low until late afternoon or even until the evening. Looking about her for a shelter, she found a grove of aspens, with their leaves flashing silver when the wind struck them and a continual shiver of whispers passing through the trees. So she rode Nancy into the middle of the little wood, unsaddled her, and tied her on a long rope to graze or lie down as she pleased.

For her part, she found the deepest shadow, unrolled her blankets, and was instantly asleep.

When she wakened she was lying in a patch of yellow light; a branch snapping under the hoof of Nancy as she grazed had wakened her. Mary Hood sat up, bewildered. She had fallen asleep at about ten in the morning. It was now fully six in the evening, and the sun would be down very shortly. She had been sleeping cold for the last hour perhaps, and the rising sound of the wind promised her a chilly night indeed.

She went methodically and mechanically about her preparations for the night ride, feeling more and more the folly of this journey to an unknown end. First she looked anxiously to Nancy, examining her hoofs, looking her over with minute care, while Nancy followed her mistress about and seemed, with her sniffling nose, to have joined the inquiry. But Nancy seemed perfectly sound. And that was the most important thing just now. That, and the fact that her stomach was crying for food.

Mary was so hungry that her hand shook when she saddled the mare. She mounted and rode out of the wood. She had barely reached the open, however, when she whipped Nancy around and back into cover. Over a near-by hill jogged half a dozen horsemen, and at their head she recognized the formidable figure of Hal Dunbar.

Her first impulse was to give Nancy the spur and ride as fast and as far as she could away from the pursuers. But she was already out of the country with which she was thoroughly familiar, and she felt that even though she outdistanced the horses behind her she would eventually be caught in a long chase. Certainly Hal Dunbar would not spare money or horseflesh to catch her.

She followed a second and really braver impulse. She tethered Nancy in the center of the wood and crept back on her hands and knees, literally, to the edge of the copse. There she lay in covert and watched the coming of the horsemen. Her father was not among them, by which she was given to understand that he had taken other groups of men to hunt in different directions. But the rat-faced Riley, the close lieutenant and evil genius of Hal Dunbar, was among those who now brought their horses from a lope to a stand not twenty yards away.

It seemed to the girl that when once any pair of those keen eyes turned in her direction they would pierce through her screen of leaves and reveal her. But though many eyes turned that way, and she shrank in mortal fear each time, no one came closer.

"You see it's what I told you," Hal Dunbar was saying. "She didn't come this way, and if she did she'd have ridden a lot farther. That would be her instinct, to jump on Nancy and ride like mad until the mare dropped. No sense in a woman. She wouldn't have the brains to cache herself away for the day and start on again at night."

The girl smiled faintly to herself.

"You're the boss," said Riley sullenly. "But I think she's got more brains that you credit her with, and if I was you, I'd search every hollow and cave and clump of trees and old shack you can find right about in here. This is the distance she most likely went if she stopped a little after it was full day. If I was you, I'd begin and hunt through that bunch of aspens."

"All right, go ahead and search through 'em."

Mary Hood cast a frantic glance back toward Nancy. She could reach the horse in time to spur on ahead of the pursuers, but she found suddenly that fear had stolen the strength from her body, and a leaden heart weighed her down.

"Wait a minute," called Hal Dunbar as Riley started toward the trees. "No use doing fool things like that. We'll ride for White Pine to-night. That'll be a good starting place for us to-morrow. No, I'll go to White Pine. Riley, you'd better take the trail to the Hollow. And, remember, you and the rest of the boys, when you see her, go out and get her. If you have to be rough, be rough. If you can't stop her without dropping her horse, shoot! I'll be responsible if any danger happens to the girl in the fall. But I'm not going to have that ungrateful slip get away from me. Understand?"

They nodded silently and gloomily.

"And the lucky fellow who gets her for me will have nothing more to worry about in life. Understand? I'll take care of him."

She watched them nod one by one—sober, gloomy-faced men. If any illusion had remained to her that these cow-punchers were fond of her, that illusion was instantly dispelled. Whatever affection they had for her, they had more for money. Bitterly she recognized in this the result of the hand picking of her father. Now the group split and rode in opposite directions.

CHAPTER XXVI

RELIEF

THEY spread, as though fate had directed them, to the right and left of the northern course which she had mapped out for herself. Lucky for her that cunning Riley did not have his way! She feared and hated the man for his insight, and lest he should turn back to take a look at that grove of aspens as soon as the big boss was out of the way, she no sooner saw both groups of horsemen out of sight than she swung into the saddle and sent Nancy flying down the hollow toward the north.

A two minutes' ride brought her into another copse, well away, and, reining there, she turned and saw that Riley had indeed turned back toward the grove with his three companions. He disappeared into it. Presently she heard his shouting.

She waited for no more but gave Nancy the rein again and fled on straight north. She had no immediate fear. Riley had found the impression of her body in the soft mold under the trees, and certainly he had found the sign of Nancy. More than that, he would doubtless be able to read her trail running north and follow it swiftly, but he and his men rode tired horses which had been urged hard all through the day, and she herself was on a runner as fresh as the wind. Moreover, the night would soon come and blot out the trail for them.

It was unlucky, of course. It meant that they had

picked up the direction of her flight, at least, and
they would follow hard, buying new horses when they
rode out the ones they were on at present. Yet too
much hurry would spoil her game. Besides, she was
weak from hunger and felt that she dared not risk
collapse on her own part by hard riding. In thirty
hours she had had only a bite of food.

When she dismounted at a water hole to let Nancy
drink, she herself went to the pure trickle of water
that ran into the pool. The taste of the water made
her head spin. Certainly she must have nourishment
before long or she could not keep the trail.

A squirrel scolded at her from a branch above.
The girl looked up at the delicate little creature
hungrily. Looking coldly and calmly at it she forgot
that she had always been horrified in the past when
men shot these pretty little things out of the trees.
Hunger and flight were deeply changing Mary Hood.

She dared not fire a shot. There was no sound
among the hills behind her, no neigh of horses, no
clangor of iron-shod hoofs against the rocks. But
she knew that the pursuit was coming slowly and
surely behind her, and she must not help them along
with such sign posts as rifle shots, or even the report
of a revolver. The little .32 which she had balanced
in her palm she shoved back into the holster and
climbed again into the saddle and went on. Still as
she went she looked back over her shoulder. The
squirrel sat upon his branch, quite ignorant of the
fact that he had been a small part of a second from
death, and chattered a farewell to her.

Then the evening closed darkly around her, and
they began to climb rapidly toward the summit. It
was the weariest time in the girl's life. She dared

not think of food now, because it brought an almost irresistible desire to weep and complain, and she felt that tears would be a foolish waste of necessary strength.

Nancy went valiantly and skillfully about her work, but cat-foot though she was, she stumbled again and again. It was a wretched excuse for a trail that they were following, and moreover it was all strange country to Nancy. She was used to the sweeping, rolling lands of the Dunbar ranch, where a horse could gallop with never a care for her footing. She was much at a loss among these ragged rocks.

It must have been about eleven o'clock when they got over the summit and saw the mass of dark ranges pitching down before them. The loftier masses of darkness against the stars, far north, were the Tompson Mountains. She might reach their foothills in the morning if she were lucky.

Now, with Nancy laboring down a slope, the eye of the girl caught the wink of a camp fire in the midst of the trees. A thousand thoughts of food rushed into her mind. A banquet or a crust of bread? She hardly knew which she would prefer, and straightway she sent Nancy scampering recklessly toward that cheerful spot of light.

All at once the light went out. Mary Hood reined the horse with a groan. She was in country now where she could not be known. But this covering of a camp fire at the sound of an approaching traveler was not an auspicious sign. Many a ruffian, she knew, sought a refuge from the punishment of the law among the Tompson Mountains and the neighboring ranges with their intricate tangles of ravines.

Sadly the girl swung her mare's head to the right. In vain Nancy tossed her head. For fear lest the mare whinny, Mary reached over and tapped the muzzle of the bay, and Nancy, as though she understood that silence was desired, merely snorted softly, and went on sullenly with ears flattened.

She was a company-loving horse, was Nancy, and she had caught the scent of companions of her own kind, no doubt, for the wind was blowing toward them from the place where Nancy had first seen the spot of light. The wind was coming toward them and it blew—— Mary Hood reined her horse sharply! Of all tantalizing scents in the world there is none to the hungry man like the fragrance of frying bacon, and that was the odor which came richly down the wind to Mary until her mouth watered and her brain reeled.

At once she forgot all caution. She wheeled Nancy and rode straight toward that scent. If there was danger she would meet it gladly, but first she must have some rashers of that bacon. However grim these men might be, they would not refuse a woman food.

Yet they might guess her a man, perhaps a pursuer on their trail, and so she began to call as she came closer, hallooing clearly through the woods till faint echoes came back to her from the higher slopes.

Still she saw nothing; she was riding through the utter black of the night. And then, under her very nose, some one said: "Pile up the fire again, boys. It's a woman."

Then a tongue of flame was uncovered—they had

framed the fire with a blanket and a dry branch thrown upon it filled the wood around her with uncertain waves of light. It made the whole scene wild beyond description, but wilder than the strange old trees were the three men who now walked boldly into the light of the fire.

It was not their size that dismayed her, for though they were all stalwart six-footers they were nothing to the giant bulk of Hal Dunbar or Bull Hunter. But the faces of these men made her quake, and forgetting all thought of hunger, she wished suddenly to flee. Yet flight would be more fearful than to stay and face the danger bravely. For they were not men to be eluded if they wished for any reason to detain her.

A family likeness united the three men of the mountains. All were of one stature, tall and gaunt and wide of shoulder, powerful and tireless men, she could guess. All had streaming hair, uncut for months, and their lean faces were covered with scraggly beards. But the hair of one was gray —she guessed him to be a man of fifty—and the black-haired fellows beside him were doubtless his sons.

All three looked at her from under heavy scowling brows with little bright eyes. They were armed to the teeth with revolvers and hunting knives, and their rifles leaned against the trees around the fire in convenient reaching distance. Their gestures habitually strayed to their weapons, fondling the butts of the revolvers, or toying with the knives, or idly fumbling with the rifles.

Even a child would have known that these men did not keep the law. Their eyes were never still;

their heads were forever turning; and everything
spoke of that restlessness of men who are hunted
by men. The fear of an outraged society was upon
them.

No matter how much she wished to retreat now,
it was too late. The hand of the father fell on the
bridle rein of Nancy and drew the mare with her
burden toward the fire, and the two tall sons closed in
from either side. They seemed doubly formidable
at this close range. Mary Hood could not move.
Her arms hung limp, her head sank.

The two boys spoke not a word. But they drew
close to her with grins of strange pleasure. One
of them took her nerveless hand in his huge, grimy
paw, and, lifting it, he showed it to his brother and
laughed foolishly. The other touched her dress,
smiling into her face with eyes that flickered like
lightning from feature to feature and back again.
She thought them half-witted, or entirely mad.

"Hey, Harry, Joe!" cried the father. "What
d'you mean starin' the lady out of face like that?
Been a long time since they seen a girl, and they
mostly don't know how they should act, but they'll
come around. Don't look so scared at 'em. They
ain't going to do you no harm! Here, climb outn
your saddle and sit down and rest yourself."

It was the sweetest of sweet music to the girl,
these hurried words, together with the sharp reproof
to the two big fellows. She got out of the saddle,
but faltered the moment her heels struck the ground.
She was weaker than she had thought. The old
man was instantly beside her and had his arms beneath her shoulders.

"Get some water. Don't stand there like idiots,"

he called to Joe and Harry. "Step alive or I'll skin you. The lady's sick. Sit here, ma'am. Now rest yourself against that log. Wait till I get a blanket. There you are. Put your hands out to that fire. Heaven a'mighty, if you ain't plumb fagged!"

The kindness was so unexpected, so hearty and genuine, that tears welled up in the eyes of the girl as she smiled at the wild woodsman. He squatted beside her patting her hands.

"I know. You got lost. Been riding a couple of days and nothing to eat. Well, these hills would bother most anybody. But wait till I get a cup or two of coffee into you and a few slices of—hey, Joe, lay your knife into that bacon and get some off —and cut it thin! I know the way a lady likes her chuck!"

CHAPTER XXVII

GOOD NEWS

AT least the cooking of Sam, as he said he was
called, was better, she was willing to vow,
than any she had ever tasted. What matter if the
bacon was fat and cut thick in spite of his in-
junctions, and the flapjacks unspeakably greasy, and
the ample venison steak only half done, and the
coffee bitter beyond imagining. It was food, and
her blood grew rich and warmly contented again
as she ate.

Sam himself sat cross-legged beside her and
a little to the front, overseeing all the operations
of that meal, applauding each mouthful she took
with a smile and a nod, and eagerly following the
motions of her hand as though he himself were
half starved and the food she ate were nutriment to
him.

As for the two gaunt sons, they were kept busy
following the orders of their father to bring new
delicacies for the girl, or to build up the fire, or
to unsaddle her horse, or to cut evergreen boughs
for her bed that night and lay it in a comfortable
place beside the fire.

They obeyed these instructions with a sort of
hungry eagerness that amazed her. She began to
be surprised that she had ever feared them. When
they had done anything for her comfort they stole
small, abashed side glances at her and flushed under

her answering smile. They were like half-wild puppies, fearing the hand of man but loving the touch of it. Her heart welled up in pity of them and their ragged clothes and their fierce, lean faces, grown mature before their time.

"Just think of how you near missed us," said Sam, as the meal reached an end at length. "When we heard your hoss come up the wind I had the boys douse the fire. Never can tell in these parts. Wild folks are about ready to do wild things, and old Sam ain't the one to be took by surprise. No, sir!"

He watched her face keenly and covertly to discover any doubt of the truth of his words.

"I don't think you are," replied Mary Hood. "The fire went out by magic, it seemed to me. And I only blundered on it again by chance."

"You see?" said Sam triumphantly to the two sons. "That's what I tell you all the time." He turned to the girl again. "Joe and Harry always want to leave the fire burning and slip off among the trees. If anybody comes up to snoop around the fire, then it's hunter hunt hunter. And there you are. But my way is best. Never take no chances. Keep away from trouble. Run from a fight. That's my way of doing things. In spite of all that, you'll find trouble enough in this world!"

He continued to watch her while he talked. She answered his glance with difficulty, looking gravely and steadily into his face. Presently he laughed, embarrassed.

"Now, we're a rough-looking lot ourselves," he continued. "What might you take us to be, lady? You ain't told us your name yet."

"My name is Mary Hood." Why conceal the name, she thought.

"Mary Hood? That's a pretty plain name for a girl like you. But going back where I stopped, how might you make us out, Mary Hood?"

She sighed. It might infuriate them if she told the truth; but if she lied they would soon suspect her dissimulation.

"I only guess, of course," she said softly. "You are men who have been very kind to me, and of course I like you for your kindness. You are prospectors, perhaps, in the mountains."

"You make us out that way, eh?" said the old man, rubbing his hands together. "Hear that, boys? This lady has an eye, eh?"

She added slowly: "And I think that perhaps you are also fugitives from the law. I don't know. I only guess. But I'm afraid you're unhappy fellows, and the law hunts you."

The three men became three moveless statues looking gravely at her, not with anger or sullen spite, but as men who have been judged and cannot appeal from the judgment.

The old man changed the subject. "How come you to get lost?"

She paused to think. If she told him that she had indeed lost her way there were nine chances in ten that he would discover the lie before he had talked with her for five minutes. But if she confessed everything she might win him to her side, and then whoever followed her trail to these men would get no further clews from them.

"I am running away," she said simply.

At a stride the two tall youths came near with

their great shadows standing boldly against the trees behind them. They looked earnestly down into her face as though by her confession she had been drawn closer to them. They, the fugitives, could understand the pursued.

Sam was chuckling. "You had a little change of words with the gent you're engaged to marry, maybe, and got so mad you figured you'd leave and never see him again? Was that it?"

His random guess had struck so close to the truth that she stared at him.

"Maybe I hit it the first time," he said, nodding. "Yes, I guess I pretty near did."

"Very nearly. But the whole truth is that I have a very stern father."

"H'm. I've heard tell of such things before, but mostly the fathers I've seen has been stern just to do good to their boys and their girls."

He pointed the moral of his tale with a meaning glance at the two youths.

"I think so," she confessed; "but sometimes they may be wrong. This father of mine wants me to marry a man I don't love."

"H'm," said Sam, nodding. "But maybe you could get to love him? Has he got money and looks and——"

"Everything," she said frankly.

"But you're kind of fond of somebody else, most like?"

"Yes."

"What sort is he?"

"An outlaw."

The three stared at her, each with parted lips. "How come?" said Sam softly.

Mary's voice rose a little. "Because a friend of his was in jail, and he went and broke into that jail and brought his friend out."

There was a gasp—of relief perhaps—from the three.

"He ain't any gun fighter, then?"

"No, he's as gentle as a child!"

"But he busts into jails, eh?" said Sam smilingly. "Well, that sounds kind of queer, but they ain't any use judging a man till you've seen him, and it's better to wait till you've watched him work. But you've talked pretty straight to me, Mary Hood."

"Because I think you can help me and will help me," said the girl.

"Maybe," he said, nodding. "To get to this man you're bound for?"

"Yes. Perhaps you know him. A very big man, Charlie Hunter——"

"Never heard tell of him."

"And a very little man called Pete Reeve."

"Pete Reeve!" cried Sam. "Him?" His face darkened, but finally he drove his angry memories away.

"You do know him?"

"Sure I know him," said Sam gloomily. "Him and me has tangled, and he got all the luck of the draw that day. Some time maybe——" He paused abruptly. "But this ain't helping you. You turn in and sleep the sleep of your life now, and when the morning comes I'll point out the way to you. I come on the trail of Pete Reeve yesterday."

Mary Hood was sitting up, smiling with happiness. All her worries were on the verge of being solved, it seemed, by this veteran of the wilderness.

"How could you tell that it was his trail when you crossed it?"

"By the way his noon fire was built. Fires is made as many different way as clothes. Some likes 'em small and heaped to a point, and some likes 'em wide, and some lays 'em to windward of rocks, and some is just as happy when they can get a place in the lee of a hill. Well, I come on Pete Reeve's fire and knowed it as well as I know his face. Not having none too much good will for Pete—you see I talk as straight to you as you talk to me, Mary Hood—I took the trail on Reeve for a while and seen that he had a big man on a big hoss with him. I just done those things because it was like dropping in on Reeve and having a chat with him without the trouble of talking, reading his trail like that. And I seen the way he was pointing his course before I turned back and took my own way. I think I can point him out to you within a mile of where he'll be in the morning."

CHAPTER XXVIII

OLD ARROWHEAD

SHE slept that night as she had never slept before. With the sense of danger gone, the happy end of the trail made her relax in body and mind. When she wakened the sun was already in the tree tops, and the men had been up long since. Nancy came out from among the trees to whinny a soft inquiry after the well-being of her mistress.

Breakfast was a liberal feast, and then Sam took her out from the clump of trees and pointed out her way. She had stolen close up on the Tompson Mountains during her ride of the night before. Sam pointed out one bald-headed monster of a peak high above the rest.

"They were aimed for Old Arrowhead Mountain," he said. "Which it's a hard trail and a long trail, but hardest of all and longest of all for another gent to follow. I dunno what's a better way of bothering a sheriff and a posse than to take the trail up Old Arrowhead. But I'll tell you how you'll most like get to Pete Reeve and the man you want. Old Arrowhead is split right in two with a gully about twenty feet wide and a thousand deep, pretty near. Them twenty feet is crossed with a bridge, and they's only one bridge. The way to it is right up to the top of that shoulder. You aim a straight line for it and ride out your hoss an' they's a good chance that you'll get to 'em before they cross, unless it come that they make a pretty early start. Of course they may not be laying for Old Arrowhead at all. I can't read their minds, but yesterday afternoon late it sure looked that was what they was heading for."

He said good-by to her and brushed away her thanks.

In half an hour the little mare was commencing the ascent of Old Arrowhead. It was distinct in the range. It was bigger and more barren, a great crag of granite, so to speak, thrust in the midst of beautiful, forest-bearing summits. It was hard footing for a man and very bad footing indeed for a horse. Even the mountain sheep, those incomparable climbers, were not very frequent visitors in the regions where Old Arrowhead soared above timber line, a bare, black mountain whose stones were polished by the storms.

The girl kept Nancy true to her work, however, for now the sun was rolling higher and higher in the sky, and unless Reeve and Charlie Hunter wanted a ride in the heat of the day, they would start from their camp at once—if indeed they had ridden this way at all.

Now that she felt she was close to them she began to wonder more and more how she could face them with her story. Above all, Bull Hunter might be changed from the simple, lovable fellow she had known; the taint of the lawless life he had been forced to lead might be in him, for all she knew. There were a thousand possibilities and each one of them was gloomier than the other.

But there was no sign of smoke above her, which made her more and more certain that Sam Dugan had been wrong, and the two had not ridden this way at all. For the very reason that she doubted, she pressed Nancy the more until the brave little mare was stumbling and sweating in her labor up the steep slope.

As the girl worked up the slope in this manner the first news of Charlie Hunter came down to her. It was nothing she saw, but a great voice that boomed and rolled and thundered above her. It was so great a voice that when she shouted joyously in answer, her voice was picked up and washed away in the torrent of sound.

The singing grew greater rapidly, as she drew closer. Finally she could make out that the sound was double. A thin, weak, straining voice ran like a rough thread in the huge singing of Bull Hunter. The girl smiled to herself as she hurried on.

She came on a picture that turned her smile to laughter. The camp fire was smoldering without smoke to the windward of two big rocks; the breakfast had been cooked and eaten, and the two companions sat together with their shoulders braced against boulders and sang a wild ballad to begin the day.

Mary Hood paused to marvel at the carelessness with which these two hunted men exposed themselves. In the first place, they had allowed her to come right up to them, unseen; in the second place they were not even close to their horses, which roamed about nibbling the grass fifty yards away— one a small cow pony and the other a black giant close to seventeen hands tall and muscled in proportion. Diablo was a fresh marvel to Mary Hood each time she saw the horse.

A moment later, as she swung out of her saddle, the eye of Pete Reeve discovered her. His mouth froze over the next sound, and with staring eyes of wonder he continued for another instant to beat the measure. Then he came to his feet with a shout.

"Mary Hood!" he called, running to her. "Mary Hood!"

She let him take both her hands, but her eyes were for the giant who had come to his feet with almost as much speed as his companion. There, on the side of the mountain, with only the empty blue sky to frame him, he seemed mightier of limb than ever. Then he came slowly, very slowly, toward her, his eyes never shifting.

"Mary," he kept saying, "how have you come, and why have you come?"

"Heavens, man," cried Pete Reeve, stamping in his anger and disgust, "when your lady rides about a thousand miles through a wilderness to see you, are you going to start in by asking questions? If you want to say good morning, go take her in your arms. Am I right, Mary Hood?"

Somewhere in her soul she found the courage to murmur: "You are!" But aloud she said: "I've run away, Charlie, and there was only one place in the world I could go—and that was to you."

His bewilderment was changing gradually to joy, and then full understanding came upon that slow mind. He checked a gesture as though he would sweep her into his arms, and instead he raised her hand and touched it with his lips.

She loved him for that restraint. He had changed indeed from the Bull Hunter she had first known, growing leaner of face and more active of eye.

He looked years older, and it seemed to the girl that in his eye there was a touch of that same restless light she had noted in the faces of the Dugan men. The brand of the hunted was being printed on him.

Now he drew her to a place sitting between them, and the questions poured out at her. So she told all the story, only lightening the blame on her father for shame's sake. But when she came to the story of the Dugans, Pete Reeve exclaimed: "I never knew he had it in him. I've had the hatchet out for Dugan ten years. Here's where I bury it."

"Heaven only knows," said Charlie Hunter, when the story was ended, "what I've done to deserve you, but now that you're here, I'll keep you, Mary, to the end of things. Not even Hal Dunbar can take you away while I have Pete Reeve to help. I'd given you up forever. We were going to ride north and get into a new country where neither of us is known. But the three of us can do the same thing. Can you stand the hard travel, Mary?"

Mary Hood laughed, and that was answer enough.

"We can't keep on the trail we started," explained Pete Reeve. "I'll show you why."

He took her to the edge of the gulch of which Sam Dugan had spoken. It was a full twenty-five feet across and a perilous drop between sheer walls of over eight hundred feet. Once a narrow bridge had been hung across the gorge, now she could see, far below, the broken remnants of it.

"We've got to go back and climb around to the right. Costs another day's work, the breaking of this little bridge."

"But why do you keep your camp so carelessly?"

asked the girl. "Any one could have surprised you just as I did."

"No enemy could," answered Pete Reeve. "There's our guard, and he can't be beat."

He pointed to a great, gray-coated dog who lay stretched at full length among the rocks a little farther down the hill.

"The Ghost knew you," said Reeve, "or he would of give us warning while you were a thousand yards away. Now we'll have to pack up and hurry."

"Somehow," murmured the girl, "I don't like the thought of turning back. It seems unlucky."

"We got to," answered Pete Reeve, "because we got to make a big circle and come through Patterson City and get a minister. Then we can hit north again."

To this, of course, she had no reply.

CHAPTER XXIX

THE SIGN

WHEN Sam Dugan came back to his camp he gave quick orders.

"Get the shovel, Joe," he commanded, "and cover that fire. We done a fool thing in starting it in plain daylight. That smoke can be seen about five miles away. Get the hosses ready, Harry. We mooch out of here as fast as we can. We sure stayed too long."

Indeed, they had never lighted a fire in broad daylight for many a month, but for the sake of Mary Hood they had broken that time-honored custom. When the father saw that the preparations were well under way, he stepped to the edge of the circle of trees and walked around it, keeping an anxious watch on the hill tops and the big, swift slopes of the mountains.

Presently, over a southern crest, he saw four horsemen riding straight for the trees.

"Quick," he shouted to his sons. "We got to run for it!"

But as he turned back into the trees again his eyes flashed toward the west, and he made out a scattering half dozen more hard riders breaking out of a grove. It was easy to see that the Dugans had been surrounded, and that the aim of all those men was the group of trees from which the smoke had been seen to rise. He made his resolution at once and went back to tell it to his sons.

"They got us dead to rights," he said quietly. "They's ten men in sight and maybe ten more coming after them. Boys, we might make a long stand in these trees and hold 'em off, but they could starve us to death. They's just one chance we got agin' bad luck, and that is that these gents ain't on our trail. If they don't know us, it's all right. If they do know us, we're lost. Now go straight ahead with your packing up, but take it slow. When they's a bunch of gents around asking questions it's always a good thing to have plenty to keep your hands busy with. These folks will be here pronto—they're here now. I'll do the talking!"

Even as he spoke, the first of the riders crashed through the shrubbery beyond the trees, and a moment later, from every side, ten grim-faced men were in view surrounding the little clearing where the camp fire had burned.

They discovered old Sam Dugan in the act of tamping down the tobacco in his corncob pipe. He continued that work and even lighted the pipe while the leader of the newcomers was speaking. He was such a man as Sam Dugan had never seen. He and his tall sons were dwarfed by the mighty dimensions of this man. The stout gray horse from which he dismounted was downheaded from the weariness of bearing that load. He had been riding long and hard, and the lines of continued exertion had made his handsome face stern.

He looked Sam Dugan fiercely up and down.

"We've come on a trail that points pretty straight toward this camp fire you've just put out so quickly," he said. "We want to know if you've seen a girl pass this way. A very pretty girl riding a bay mare.

Sam Dugan stopped and rubbed his knuckles through his beard in apparent thought.

"Girl on a bay mare. I dunno, I dunno. Boys, you ain't seen anybody like that around in sight? Nope, I guess we ain't seen her, partner. Sorry about it. Runaway, maybe?"

His calm seemed to madden the big stranger, but the latter controlled an outburst.

"Look here, my friend," he continued, "I'm Hal Dunbar. I'm a little outside of my own country, but if you were down there they'd tell you that I'm a man of my word, and I promise you that if you have seen that girl in passing and can give me any idea where she's gone, I'll make it mighty well worth your while to talk."

"Well," said Sam Dugan genially, "that sounds to me like pretty easy money, and if I could get hold on it I sure would. But when I don't know I can't very well tell, and I guess that's about all that there is to it."

"H'm," said Dunbar growlingly. "It looks that way. But bad luck is certainly following me on this trail. However, we'll keep trying. Heads up, boys. We've got a lot more riding before us, it seems, and I hoped that this might be the end of the trail."

Jack Hood tapped his friend Riley on the arm. "There's something a bit queer about it," he said to Riley. "That fire was burning high just a minute ago. Look at that stick poking out through the dirt. It ain't half charred. That fire wasn't burned out by no means. But inside of five minutes they

got that fire covered and their packs about made up.
I admit there ain't very much in those packs, but
still it's fast work. And now them two long, lanky
gents are lazying along as if they didn't have any
hurry at all in mind. Looks to me, Riley, like the
three of them made up their minds for a quick start
a while back, and then changed their minds pronto.
Talk to 'em, Riley."

The latter nodded. Big Hal Dunbar was turning
away gloomily when Jack Hood stopped him with a
signal.

"Might get down and give the hosses a spell,
chief, eh?" suggested Riley to Dunbar, and the
latter, receiving the wink from Jack Hood, nodded.
Instantly the crew was on the ground lolling at
ease.

"Been long on the trail?" asked Riley, fixing his
shoulders comfortably against the trunk of a tree.

"Tolerable long," said Sam Dugan, steady in his
rôle of the silent man.

"Been coming down from the north, maybe?"

"Yep, coming down from the north."

"We're up from the south," volunteered Riley.
"My name's Riley. This is Jack Hood."

He named all those present. Then he paused.
The challenge was too direct to be passed.

"Glad to meet you gents," returned Sam Dugan.
"My name's Sam Saunderson, and these two are my
boys, Joe and Harry."

The latter turned and grinned at the strangers.

"You been prospecting coming down, I figure,"
said Riley, glancing at the packs.

"Nothing particular," said Sam Dugan. "Raised

color a couple of times. That was all. Nothing particular much to talk about."

"What part you start from?"

"Might say I didn't start from nowheres; me and the boys have been traveling for so long we don't hardly stop much anywhere."

It was dexterous fencing, and done, withal, with such consummate ease that Riley could not tell whether the old fellow was making a fool of him or telling the truth. He shrewdly suspected the former, but pinning down Sam Dugan was like pinning down another old man of the sea. He was slippery as oil.

"Mostly mining?" he suggested.

"Oh, I dunno. Ain't much that I ain't turned a hand to for a spell, take it all in all."

"But liking to follow the rocks, I guess you been around the Twin River Mines, maybe?"

"Sure, I've dropped by 'em."

"How long back?"

"Oh, long about five year back, I guess, or maybe it was only three. I dunno. Dates and things like that get out of my head pretty easy."

"If you was there five year back, I guess you knew Jud Chalmers, maybe?"

"Guess maybe I did. Think I remember having a drink with a gent by that name."

"The Jud Chalmers I know don't drink," said Riley, his eyes brightening.

"Well, well, he don't?" said mild Sam Dugan. "Come to think about it, I guess it was a gent named Jud Chambers I had that drink with."

"Maybe you knew Cartwright up there?"

"Cartwright? Lemme see. Well, I'll tell you

a funny story about a gent by name of Cartwright. It was back in——"

Riley sighed. He had thought a moment ago that he was cornering this ragged mountaineer, but Sam Dugan had skillfully wound out of a dangerous corner and come into the clear again. It was useless to try to corner a man who told stories. It was like trying to drink all the water in a lake to get at a bright pebble on the bottom of it. After all, the man was probably entirely innocent of having seen Mary Hood. Riley gave up, and in sign that he had surrendered he rose and yawned and stretched himself.

"I guess we're fixed, ain't we, Joe?" asked Sam Dugan.

Jack Hood's eye had been caught by something beneath a dry log at one side of the clearing. He crossed to it.

"All fixed," answered Joe Dugan.

"Sorry to leave you, gents," went on Sam Dugan. "But I'm leaving you a right good camp. Got good water over yonder, and there's all the wood and forage an army would want. Get my hoss for me, Harry. So long, gents. Sure hope you find the girl, stranger."

So speaking, waving genially to each of them as he passed, Sam Dugan sauntered across the clearing, leading his horse. The call of Jack Hood stopped him as he was about to disappear among the trees. He turned and saw the foreman of the Dunbar ranch standing with his hands on his hips.

"You say you ain't seen my daughter, eh?"

"That girl you was talking about? Well?"

"How long have you been in this here camp?"

"Oh, about a day."

"Then," said Jack Hood, "I got to tell you that my daughter has been here, and she sure has been here inside of twenty-four hours, and she sure couldn't of come without being seen."

"That's kind of hard talk, ain't it?" said Sam Dugan, feeling that a crisis had come.

"It sure is, but it's straight talk. Maybe you got your own reasons for not talking. I dunno what they are, but they sure ain't any good. Here's all the sign I want that she was here."

And he raised a hand in which fluttered a filmy bit of white, the handkerchief of a girl.

CHAPTER XXX

HOT PURSUIT

WITH a triumphant yell, Hal Dunbar shot across the clearing and caught at the handkerchief as though it had been the girl herself. Then he turned furiously on Sam Dugan.

"Now," he said, "will you talk?"

"It kind of looks like I'd been doing a lot of lying that got me nowheres in particular," said Sam Dugan, grinning and quite unabashed. "But still I don't figure any particular call I got to talk. Not by a pile. So long, gents."

But as he turned, Hal Dunbar, with a leap, barred his way. It was a hard trial for Sam Dugan. It was not the first time he had been halted, but it was the first time the rash intruder had escaped unscathed. Now the odds were too greatly against him, and though Sam Dugan loved a fight above all things in the world, he loved best of all a fight which he had a chance of winning. Moreover, he guessed shrewdly that this man alone would be more than a match for him.

"Saunderson," said Hal Dunbar grimly, "or whatever your name is, I've been on this trail for a long time, and there are twenty other men riding it with me. I'm going to keep them riding till the trail comes to an end. That girl is going to be found. Why not speak up like a man and tell me what way she went?"

"You got eyes to find that trail, ain't you?" asked Dugan savagely.

"Mind your tongue," said Hal Dunbar, his eyes instantly on fire. "Look around at these mountains. Chopped up like the waves in a wind. I could spend a month hunting over ten square miles unless I have a lead to follow with my men."

"That sounds like sense," said Sam Dugan, and he spoke more kindly now. He liked the fact that the big man had not yet threatened him with the power of numbers, and he liked the big, clean look of Hal Dunbar.

A moment later he was being tempted as he had never been tempted before.

"Why do you cover her trail?" asked Dunbar.

"Because she asked me to."

"If a runaway child of six asked you not to tell where it had gone, would you keep the promise?"

"But she's a pile more'n six, my friend."

"She's not more able to take care of herself."

"That may be true, but she's going to one who will."

"An outlaw," said Hal Dunbar hotly. "A fellow she's only seen three times. It makes me turn cold when I think about it! Suppose she marries him— though Heaven knows how they can ever get to a minister—what would come of their life? What of their children?"

This blow shook Sam Dugan to the core. Hal Dunbar followed up his advantage.

"Saunderson, if that's your name, you're saving that girl if you tell me how I can follow her. I've an idea that in certain places you may be wanted, my friend. I think that the sheriffs, any of them, would be very much interested if I brought in you and your sons. Eh?"

Dugan watched him narrowly, decided that the big fellow could do it if he wished, and then determined that he would make his last stand here, rather than be so ignominiously captured. Yet he would avoid the blow as long as he could. He was greatly relieved by the next words of Hal Dunbar.

"I could take you and your boys along. You look suspicious. You must have bought those clothes five years ago, and yet you've been traveling for five hundred miles near towns. Very queer. But instead of forcing you, I'm going to do the opposite. Saunderson, if that girl gets into those mountains with Hunter she's lost. No man on earth could follow her. For Heaven's sake tell me where she's gone. I love her, I tell you frankly, but I want to stop her in the first place simply to keep her from marrying an outlaw. Is she cut out for camp life like this? Answer that, Saunderson, and you know that camp life in winter——"

"Yes, you're right," said Sam Dugan gravely.

"I'll give her a home and she won't have to marry me for it. I'll swear that to you, Saunderson. I know you're only trying to do what's best for the girl, so you see I open my mind to you. Another thing—you and your two boys might need a bit of a stake. I'm the man that can fix that for you."

"How high would you go?" asked Sam Dugan curiously.

"Five thousand—ten thousand," was the unhesitating answer.

Sam Dugan sighed. Curiously enough, it was the very sum which he had set before him as a goal.

"I guess you're straight about her," said Dugan. "I figure if you'll pay ten thousand just to find her trail you sure love her, and——"

"Part of that sum I'll give you in gold. I'll give you my note for the rest and——"

"I don't want the money. I only wanted to find out if you was really fond of her, and you are. I'll show you the way. But maybe you're too late." He pointed. "Look yonder to Old Arrowhead. Ride straight for the center of the hill, and you'll catch her trail. And ride hard."

A muffled shout from Hal Dunbar, and he was in the saddle on the weary gray. His men followed him with less alacrity. Sam Dugan, however, watching them stream out of the grove and across the open country, shook his head as he turned back to his two sons.

"Word breaking don't generally bring no good to nobody," he said doubtfully. "Maybe I've been all wrong to tell the big chap. But I done what I thought was right."

Meantime Hal Dunbar was urging his men on with shouts. For the gray could not keep pace. Only fox-faced Riley drew back beside the big boss.

"There's a gorge up there and a small bridge across it," he said. "If they get across that and have time to break down the bridge, we're done for."

Hal Dunbar groaned and returned no answer except by spurring his horse cruelly. The gray, attempting in vain to increase his speed, stumbled and staggered and then went on with greater labor than ever. His head was hanging, his sides working like bellows, and the noise of his breathing was a horrible, bubbling, rasping sound. Riley, with a glance, knew that the gray was being ridden to death, but he said nothing. Advice, when Hal was in one of his furies, only maddened him the more.

Meantime they were working up the hill rapidly.

"They've sighted us," called Riley at length; "and if they start for the bridge we can never stop them."

"Where are they?" asked Hal Dunbar, ceasing for the instant his steady labor of flogging the gray and spurring him on.

"Up yonder. There's their guard!"

He pointed to a gray streak, moving with incredible speed and smoothness across the face of the hill.

"The Ghost," replied Hal Dunbar with a significant nod. "The beast is their outpost, eh." He groaned as he spoke. "One last try, boys!" he yelled to his men. "Drive the horses. We've only got seconds left to us!"

He suited his actions to his words by spurring the gray again, but that honest horse had given the last of his strength already and had been running on his nerve alone for some time, crushed by the huge burden of Hal Dunbar. Now he threw up his head as though he had been struck and fell like a clod.

He dropped straight down, and Dunbar, unhurt, kicked his feet out of the stirrups and ran on, cursing. There was no pity for the horse in him, only a wild anger that he should be hampered at such an hour even by the horseflesh which he rode. But he had not taken a dozen steps when a rifle exploded far up the slope, and a bullet hummed wickedly past him, yet it was far above his head.

"Shall we rush 'em?" he called to Riley.

"Rush Pete Reeve?" said the other sneeringly. "I'd as soon rush dynamite. Get the boys to cover."

He was following his own suggestion as he spoke, and the rest of the men needed no order. They dived from their horses and took up their positions behind the big rocks which littered the side of Old Arrowhead Mountain. Riley found a place close to the ranch owner.

"I dunno what's happened," he said. "They ought to be across that bridge by now, but they ain't. Listen!"

The rifle snapped above them again, and one of the men cursed as the bullet splashed on the rock above his head.

"He's just shooting to warn us that he means trouble," interpreted Riley. "When Reeve shoots to kill he either kills or he doesn't shoot at all. Ain't many bullets he's wasted on thin air, I can tell you. He's trying to hold us back with his lead, and that simply means that something has happened to the bridge and he can't get across it."

"Then," gloated Hal Dunbar, "I've got 'em in the hollow of my hand."

He shouted a few orders—men scampered from rock to rock until the cordon had been drawn in a perfect semicircle all the way around the crest of the hill. The three fugitives were hemmed in with only one way of escape without fight, and that way led across a twenty-five foot gorge.

"If you got a white handkerchief," said Hal Dunbar, "put it up on the end of your revolver for a flag of truce, and then go up and talk to them. Tell them that all I want is the girl. The rest of 'em can go. Tell 'em that. Also tell them that if money talks to them I'll hold as long a conversation as they want."

"D'you mean that you'd let both of 'em go if they give you the girl?"

"Sure I don't," replied Hal Dunbar, chuckling. "I only want to get her out of the way before I finish those two skunks. But make all the promises you want to make. A promise made to an outlaw isn't a promise at all, is it?"

"Maybe not—I guess not," said Riley.

And straightway he tied a white handkerchief to the end of his revolver and waved it above the rock.

There was an answering call from up the hill.

"All right!"

Riley rose and started up the slope.

CHAPTER XXXI

FACING THE ENEMY

LITTLE Pete Reeve, lying prone among the rocks at the crest of the hill and keeping a sharp outlook, reported what happened to Hunter and the girl. She had lost her courage with the firing of the first shot and sat white and sick of face, leaning into the arms of Charlie Hunter. The big man soothed her as well as he could.

"But if something happens," she kept saying, "it will all have been my fault. I laid the trail that they followed to you."

And so the voice of cunning Riley came to them from the other side of the knoll, where he had been stopped by the challenge of Pete Reeve before he should clear the top and be able to see that the bridge had actually fallen and that the three were definite and hopeless prisoners.

"Look here, Reeve," said Riley, "we know what's happened. Something's busted the bridge, and you fellows can't get over. Now, the boss doesn't care about you and Bull Hunter. He's got only one thing he's thinking about, and that's the girl. He says if you'll let her come down to him, he'll let you two go clear."

"That's something for the girl to answer, not me," answered Pete Reeve. "Keep back a bit while I talk to them."

He turned and said softly: "You've heard what

he said; maybe he means it and maybe he don't. I think he'd have his fill of fighting before he got us, but he could starve us out. That's the straight of how we stand just now. I want you to know that pretty clear. I also want you to know that there ain't one chance in a million of you or any one of us getting away. This is a tight trap. But if you want to stay, then the three of us stick, and welcome."

"There's only one answer to give him," said the girl, rising to her feet steadily enough. "Tell him that I'm coming. But first I want to hear Hal Dunbar swear to let you both go free."

"Shall I tell him that?" asked Pete Reeve.

"No," interrupted Charlie Hunter, speaking for the first time. "Tell him to go back. He gets no sight of Mary Hood."

"She'll talk up for herself, I guess," said Pete Reeve, gloomily, as he saw the one possible chance of escape slipping away from them.

"No," answered Bull Hunter solemnly. "She's come up here to me, and she's mine. I'd rather have her dead than belonging to Hal Dunbar, and she'd rather die than leave us. Is that so, Mary?"

It was the first time that either the girl or Reeve had heard the giant speak with such calm force, but in the crisis he was changing swiftly and expanding to meet the exigencies of that grim situation. He stood up now—and the little hollow at the top of the hill was barely deep enough to cover him from the eyes of the men down the slope.

"Tell him that," he continued.

"It's a crazy answer," muttered Pete Reeve. "And you've got no right to put words in her mouth."

"Every right in the world to," said the big man with the same unshaken calm. "In the first place I don't trust Dunbar. A gent that'll hound a woman the way he's hounded Mary Hood isn't worth trusting. Suppose we die? I wouldn't live a happy day in a hundred years if I knew I'd bought my life by sending Mary back to Dunbar. Pete, you know I'm right."

The little man nodded. "I couldn't help hoping it would be the other way."

"You can leave if you want to, Pete. They'll be glad to let you through. That'll make their odds still bigger."

The little man smiled. "Leave you in a pinch like this?" he said. "After what we've been through together?"

He turned sharply on Riley. The latter, during the conversation between Reeve and Bull Hunter had stolen a few paces farther up the hill until his eye came above the ridge. There across the gorge where there had once been the bridge was now empty space. Riley shrank back again, grinning and satisfied.

"You seen, did you?" asked Pete Reeve grimly. "For spying like that you'd ought to be shot down like a dog, Riley. But I'm not that kind. Go back and tell your rat of a master that we'll not let the girl go back to him. Tell him we know there's all sorts of prices for a life, but when a woman is the price then the man that lets her pay ain't man enough to be worth saving."

It had not been exactly the attitude of Pete Reeve the moment before, but, having been persuaded, he was not one to miss a rhetorical opening of this size.

Riley sneered at him. "That's what you say now," he said. "But we ain't going to rush you, Reeve. We're going to sit down and wait for the heat and the thirst to do the work with you. May take more than to-day. Then again, it may be that you'll change your mind before night. But we'll get you, Reeve, and we'll get the girl, and we'll cart your scalps to the sheriff and collect the prices on your heads. So long, Pete."

He waved his hand to them with a mocking grin and strode off down the slope.

"It's going to be a long play," he reported to his chief. "The girl won't hear no reason, or rather she lets Bull Hunter do her thinking and her talking for her. We'll have to find the nearest water and start carting it here, because the thing that's going to beat them up on the hill before night is that!"

He pointed above his head toward the sun. It was losing its morning color and rapidly becoming a blinding white. Its heat was growing every moment, and before noon the effect would be terrible, for Old Arrowhead Mountain was a mass of rock which instantly was heated along its surface until the stone burned through the soles of boots, and the reflected warmth became furnacelike.

For the circle of guards along the lower slopes, the watch through the day was bad enough, though they had the shelter of tall rocks here and there, and one of them was steadily at work bringing freshly filled canteens. But for the trio imprisoned at the top of the hill it was a day of torture.

The small basin in which they were was perfect for gathering and focusing the rays of the sun. By ten in the morning the heat had become intolerable, and still that heat was bound to increase by leaps and bounds for five hours!

Mary Hood endured the torment without a word, though her pallor increased as the time went on. There was one tall pine standing on the very verge of the cliff, but storm and lightning had blasted away most of the limbs except toward the top, and it gave them hardly any shade worth mentioning. Only in the shadow of the trunk there was room for Mary Hood, and the men forced her to stay there. Pete Reeve, withered and bloodless, endured the oven heat better than the others; Bull Hunter, suffering through all of his great bulk, went panting about the work of fanning Mary, or talking as cheerily as he could to keep her mind from the horror of their situation.

Then at noon, with the sun hanging straight above them and the heat a steady agony, unrelieved by a breath of wind, Hal Dunbar came up under another flag of truce and made a final appeal. Their reply was merely to order him back, and he went, trailing curses behind him.

That newly refused offer of help made everything seem more terrible than before. It was the last offer, they knew, that would be received from big Hal Dunbar. After that he would merely wait, and waiting would be more effective than bullets. There remained a single half pint of hot water in the bottom of Bull Hunter's canteen, and this they reserved for Mary Hood.

Twice that afternoon she tried to fight them

away, refusing the priceless liquid, but Bull Hunter forced her like a stubborn child and made her take a small swallow. But that was merely giving an edge to the thirst of the girl, and as for Hunter and Reeve, their tongues were beginning to swell. They spoke seldom, and when they did, their syllables were as thick as from drunkenness.

When the crisis of the afternoon came, between half past two and half past three, they made their decision. They would wait until full night, then they would mount their horses and ride down the slope with Mary behind them to be given shelter from the bullets. It was an entirely hopeless thought, they knew perfectly well. Such men as Jack Hood and Hal Dunbar, in particular, did not miss close shots. Those two alone could account, shooting as they would from behind perfect shelter, for a dozen men. But there was nothing else for it. The horses were gowing mad with thirst. Mary Hood was becoming feverish, and Bull Hunter was at the last of his endurance.

Wind came out of the north, at this moment, but it served rather to put the hot air in circulation than to bring any relief of coolness.

So the day wore on, and the shadows grew cooler and more blue along the sides of the tall mountain above them. There was a haven for them almost within reach of the hand, and yet they were hopelessly barred from it by the small distance across the gulch. All the time they could see the flash and sparkle of silver-running spring water on the slope not a hundred yards above them.

The shadows began to lengthen. It was impossible to find more than one shelter from the sun, and they lay at full length, praying for night. And so Bull Hunter, watching the shade of the great pine tree lengthen and stretch across the cañon, received his great idea and sat bolt erect. Thirst and excitement choked him. He could only point and gibber like a madman, and then speech came.

"Pete," he gasped out, "we've been blind all day. There's a bridge for us. You see? That pine tree can be cut down, and if it falls across the gulch we can cross it."

Pete Reeve leaped to his feet and then shook his head with a groan.

"Can't be done, Bull. That wind will knock it sidewise and it'll simply drop down into the cañon."

"It's got to be tried," said Bull Hunter, and he took his ax from his pack.

CHAPTER XXXII

THE CHASM

IT was an ax specially made for him. The haft was twice the ordinary circumference, and the head had the weight of a sledge hammer. Yet, standing with his feet braced for the work, he made the mighty weapon play like a feather about his head.

The girl and Pete Reeve sat silently to watch, not daring to speak, not daring even to hope. And so the first blow fell with power that almost buried the ax head in the wood. Then the steel was pried out with a wrench, and the second blow bit out a great chip that leaped out of sight in the void of the cañon.

After that the chips flew regularly until the tree was well nigh eaten through, and the top of it swayed crazily in the wind. Then Bull Hunter stopped, for if he continued cutting till the trunk was severed, the tree, as Pete Reeve had said, would blow sidewise in the cañon. So he waited.

"Pray for one breath of south wind," he told the others. "Pray for that. If it comes we're saved."

They nodded and sat about with their eyes glued to the top of the tree, hoping against hope that they would see the wind abate from the north and swing.

"No hope," said Bull Hunter at last. "We'd be

fools to wait for the wind to swing. Mary, lie
down there between those two rocks with your
revolver, and if you see any one show a head down
the hill, shoot as close to them as you can. Pete,
get your ax, and as soon as the wind falls off to
nothing, you start chopping, and I'll try to give
the tree a start from this side."

They obeyed him silently. Reeve stood ready
with his ax. The girl with her revolver before
her, lay between the rocks to keep watch, Bull
Hunter stood waiting for the wind to cease before
he gave the word. The Ghost, as though he realized
that the girl was taking his own old post of sentinel,
came sniffing beside her and lay down with his head
dropped on his paws, close to the head of the girl.
And big Diablo, apparently guessing that salvation
was somehow connected with the cutting of the tree,
came with his ears pricking and sniffed the raw
wound in the side of the tree. Then he backed
away to watch and wait, his eyes fixed in steady
confidence on Bull Hunter.

So, when the wind fell away for a moment, Pete
Reeve attacked the slender remnant of the trunk
which remained whole, and Bull Hunter, reaching as
far as he could up the tree, thrust with his whole
weight against it. At that angle he could do little,
but the small impulse might decide the entire direction of the fall. And so the trunk was bitter,
through, deep on the one side, and Pete Reeve, stepping around to Hunter's side of the pine, gave half
a dozen short, sharp, back strokes. There was a
great rending, and the top of the pine staggered and
began to fall.

At the same time the unlucky north wind, which

had been blowing most of the afternoon, sprang up again and swung the tree sidewise. Yet the impetus of the fall had already been received. The pine fell at a sharp angle, but it spanned the gulch from side to side. Still it was by no means a comfortable bridge. The Ghost sped across it with a bound and sat down on the far side, grinning back an invitation to follow. The three laughed in spite of themselves, but their laughter was drowned by a shout of rage down the slope.

It had taken their besiegers this time to realize the meaning of the cutting of the tree, and now, after the first yell of anger, a confused babel of voices swept up to them.

"They know what we're going to try to do," said Pete Reeve, "and they'll press us pretty close and——"

His words were interrupted by the explosion of Mary Hood's revolver, answered by a shout of mocking defiance.

"Some one tried to edge higher up the hill," she explained, through tight lips. "I hit the rock above him, and he ducked back."

"Do you think they'll try to rush?" Bull asked anxiously of little Reeve.

"They don't rush Pete Reeve in broad daylight. Nope, not if they was a hundred of 'em. The price is too high!" He waved to Bull. "I'm the lightest, and I'm next across."

"Good luck, Pete, but wait a minute. Mary goes with you. Mary!"

She came at once, but shrank back from the edge of the cañon.

"Don't look down," Reeve cautioned her. "Look

straight ahead. Look at The Ghost on the far side, and you'll keep your head. There's plenty of time. Get down on your hands and knees, and crawl. I'm here behind you. Now, steady!"

She obeyed without a word, casting one glance at Bull Hunter. Then they started, with Pete Reeve moving close behind her, waiting for a slip. But the trunk was far more firmly lodged than they had imagined. Once in the center, feeling the quiver of the tree beneath her, the girl paused, trembling, but the steady voice of Reeve gave her courage, and she went on. A moment later she was on the far side waving back to Bull Hunter.

He waved in return and then, from between the rocks, poured half a dozen shots down the slope.

"They're getting restless. That'll keep 'em for a while," Pete Reeve explained to the girl. "And now comes the hardest part for poor Charlie Hunter."

"Why the hardest part?"

"He has to leave Diablo, and that goes hard against the grain."

"Yes, I know," said the girl sadly, "just as I have to leave Nancy."

"It ain't the same," said Pete. "Diablo is more than just hoss to Bull. He's sort of a pal, too. Combination of partner and slave that's hard to beat. Look there—if the hoss don't know that Bull is giving him up."

For as Bull Hunter approached the tree trunk, the great stallion pushed in before him with ears laid flat back and made a pretense of biting him, his teeth closing on the shoulder of his master. Bull Hunter patted the velvet muzzle and stroked the forelock. Then he turned and made a gesture of despair to the two on the other side.

"I've got to go," he said, "but I can't go. Pete, I'd rather see Diablo dead than have Hal Dunbar ride him."

"There's no other way, Bull," said Reeve sadly. "And if Dunbar gets him, you'll get him back before long."

Bull Hunter shook his head, passed his hand for the last time along the smooth, shining neck of the stallion, and then stepped out on the fallen pine. Diablo, fooled by the petting of his master, wheeled and started in pursuit—but Bull Hunter was already beyond reach of his teeth. The stallion reared and struck at the thin air. Then he danced in an ecstasy of rage and disappointment, while Nancy and Reeve's horse backed as far away as possible and in amazement watched this exhibition.

Next the stallion came to the trunk and placed both forefeet upon it as though he would try to cross, though a glance into the depths below made him shrink. The sunlight trembled along his glossy coat.

"Poor devil!" muttered Pete Reeve.

But Bull Hunter had lowered his head and could not look.

"Let's start," he said. "Takes the joy out of life to leave that horse, Pete, and I'll never see him again. Dunbar won't be able to ride him, and he'll go so crazy mad that he'll kill him. I know!"

He turned away among the rocks with the girl and Reeve following in silence, but they were stopped by a great neigh from across the gulch.

They looked back with a cry of wonder coming

from every throat; and that cry was taken up and echoed along the crest on the farther side. There they stood, man after man—Jack Hood, Hal Dunbar, and all their followers.

They had rushed the crest at last only to find their quarry gone, but now they stood careless of the fact that they were exposed to the guns of Reeve and Hunter, for Diablo had ventured a step along the trunk with his head stretched out, his legs bent, his whole body trembling with terror. The wind caught his mane and tail and set them flaring. He took another step and shuddered as the trunk, beneath his great weight, settled and quaked.

"Please send him back!" said Mary Hood, catching the arm of Bull Hunter.

"Send him back," shouted Hal Dunbar, "and we'll stop the chase here. I didn't know such horses were ever bred!"

"How can he turn and go back?" called Bull Hunter in answer. "Will you let me try to help him across that tree, Dunbar?"

"Yes," he answered.

Friends and enemies, they stood ranged on either side of the gorge and watched the giant stallion's effort to gain his master back. Each step he made in mortal terror, and yet he kept on.

Bull Hunter waited for no second permission. He was instantly at the far end of the log, and at his call the gallant horse pricked his ears. They flicked back again the next moment as a gust of wind nearly knocked him from his position. But he steadied himself and made the next step. But now the trunk grew smaller and therefore less steady, and moreover, the central depth of the cañon was straight beneath him.

Then Bull Hunter stepped out on the log. His own weight helped to make the trunk less steady, but the moral effect of his coming would more than counterbalance that. Standing straight up, he placed himself in mortal danger, for the jar of one false step on the part of the horse would kill his master as well as himself. In appreciation of what was happening, Mary Hood covered her eyes, and a deep-throated murmur of applause came from the followers of Hal Dunbar on the farther side.

With short, trembling steps the big stallion moved along the trunk, and now Bull Hunter met him midway over the chasm and with his outstretched hand caught the reins close to the bit. The ears of Diablo quivered forward in recognition of this assistance. Though the powerful hand of Bull Hunter was useless, practically, to steady the great bulk of the horse, the confidence which he gave was enough to make Diablo straighten and step forward with a greater surety.

Within a yard of safety, a rear hoof slipped violently from the curved surface of the trunk, and a groan came from the anxious watchers on either side of the gulch. They had been mortal enemies the minute before. Now the heroism of the horse gave them one common interest, and they forgot all else.

The groan changed to a great gasping breath of relief as Diablo, quaking through every limb, steadied himself on the verge of reeling from the tree trunk. Here the hand and voice of Bull Hunter saved him indeed. Another step and he was on the level ground beyond, and Pete Reeve and Mary Hood and all the men of Hal Dunbar joined in one rousing shout of triumph. Diablo stood trembling beside his master, and Bull Hunter let his hand wander fondly over that beautiful head.

The noise fell away as Hal Dunbar stepped forward. He took off his hat and bowed across the chasm to Mary Hood.

"Mary," he said, "I've followed you hard, but I followed for what I thought was your own good. I didn't know Hunter then as I know him now. A man whose horse will risk death to follow him, and who will risk death to save his horse, can't be much wrong at heart. Only one thing, Mary, I want you to know. I could have stopped you here; we had Reeve and Hunter under our guns— Diablo saved them. And I want to ask you one favor in return. Ask Bull Hunter to cross the gulch and speak with me on this side for a moment. I give him my solemn word of honor that no harm will come to him from my men."

She shook her head. "I've tried you before, Hal, and I won't trust you now. I can't persuade Charlie to go—not a step."

But Bull Hunter answered: "I don't need persuading. I'll meet you on that side, Dunbar."

There was a faint cry from Mary Hood, but the big man stepped quietly onto the log and recrossed the chasm. A moment later he stood face to face with Hal Dunbar, and a murmur of awe passed over Dunbar's men. For they saw that for the first time their "big boss" was matched against a man who was his equal in size and in apparent strength.

Pete Reeve had drawn back into the shelter of a great ragged rock jutting from the mountainside, and now he called from his concealment: "I'm on guard, Dunbar. The first crooked step you take or the first suspicious move you make, I'll shoot and shoot to kill. You may drop Bull Hunter, but you'll never live to talk about it!"

Hal Dunbar bowed in mock courtesy. He had drawn Hunter aside so that their voices could not be heard by the others when they were lowered to a whispering compass.

"Dunbar," said his rival earnestly, "you've played a fair game and a square game to-day, and I'm thanking you. I don't know how you feel about it, but I'd like to shake hands. Are you willing?"

The smile which Hal Dunbar turned on him did not falter in the slightest, but what he said was: "Hunter, I hate the ground you walk on. And there's only one thing that keeps me from finishing you to-day. It's not the gun of Pete Reeve. It's the fact that Mary Hood is watching us. That's why I smile, Hunter, but I'm cursing you inside."

Bull Hunter shrugged his shoulders; there was no other answer to be made.

"I haven't asked you over here to make friends," said Hal Dunbar; "and you can rest content that there'll never be rest for either of us until one of us is dead and the other is safely married to Mary Hood. Just now she's had her head turned by you; a little later it may be my turn."

"That turn won't come," answered Bull, unshaken by the quiver of hatred that ran through the voice of the other. "She'll be married to me by to-morrow night."

Hal Dunbar closed his eyes as though a flash of sunlight had blinded him. Then he looked out again from beneath puckered brows.

"Tell me, Hunter," he said, "what'll be the outcome of that marriage? You may be happy with her for a few days, but how long d'you think it will last when you and she have to run through the mountains to keep clear of the law that follows you? Have you thought of that? And are you going to drag her with you and spoil her life because of this selfish thing you call your love for her?"

Bull Hunter paled. "I am not a very wise man, Dunbar," he said, "and I may be wrong and you may be right, but it seems to me that if a man and a woman love each other enough they have the right to take some chances."

"And if you have children?" asked Dunbar, still smiling and still savage.

Bull Hunter sighed. "I don't know," he said.

"That's why I've asked you to come and talk with me. I tell you what I can do—I have a little weight with the governor of the State. He needs financial support now and then and—but it's no use going into politics. The short of it is that the governor will do pretty much what I want him to do. Well, Hunter, suppose I were to ask him for a pardon for you; and for your friend Pete Reeve as well? Suppose I were to do that and leave you free to marry Mary Hood and settle down where you please and live your own happy lives?"

"If you did that," said Bull Hunter gravely, "you'd be the finest man that ever lived."

"But I'm not the finest. I want to know if it's

worth taking a risk to get a pardon for yourself and Reeve?"

"Any risk in the world."

"Then listen to me. I'll go back to the nearest town with a telegraph and get in touch with the governor at once. I can have your pardon wired all over the State by to-morrow morning, and you can take Mary Hood into Moosehorn before to-morrow night. You understand?"

"It's like a dream," muttered Bull Hunter.

"Here's the part of it that will wake you up again," said Hal Dunbar with his evil smile. "In Moosehorn you leave Mary Hood and come straight back toward Five Roads."

"Why?"

"Because, on the road, you'll meet me. It'll be after dark, but that doesn't make any difference. If it's dark we'll fight without guns, for a fight it's going to be, Hunter, without the girl standing by to pity you and weep over you and never forget that I killed you—you understand?"

"Yes, I begin to," said Bull Hunter. "You get me a pardon from the governor. I take Mary to safety. I come back to meet you, and one of us dies. If it is me, nothing could be better for you. You will be able to pose before Mary as having secured my pardon. It will be proof to her that you had no hand in my killing, and if I kill you, you have lost everything, indeed, and I've the guilt of killing my benefactor. Is that it?"

"Is it worth the risk?" asked the other, husky with excitement. "Think of it, Hunter! It means your chance for happiness with the girl. Do you fear me too much to meet me? I'll give you every advantage. I'll come out without a gun on me. We'll fight bare hand to bare hand. I've some skill with a gun as you know. But I'll throw that away. Do you agree?"

Bull Hunter sighed. He looked across the chasm at Mary Hood, where she stood watching him anxiously. Never had she seemed so beautiful. Yes, for the sake of her happiness it was worth risking everything. She could not lead that wandering life through the mountains.

"I'll meet you to-morrow night," said Bull Hunter. "On the way from Moosehorn to Five Roads. You have my word that I'll be there."

"Then shake hands."

"Shake hands?" said Bull huskily. "What sort of a devil are you, Dunbar? Shake hands when we intend to try to kill each other?"

"It's for the sake of the girl. It'll make her easier if she thinks that we're friends."

Bull Hunter reluctantly took the hand of the other, and then went back across the chasm to join his two companions.

CHAPTER XXXIII

SETTING THE STAGE

ALL was done punctually as the ranch owner had promised. Until late that night he kept a telegraph wire to the capitol of the State busy, and at midnight the pardons of Pete Reeve and Bull Hunter were signed, and the news was being flashed across the mountain desert.

Only one person had been with Hal Dunbar while he was doing his telegraphing, and that person was the invaluable lieutenant, Riley. The fox-faced little man blinked when he saw the contents of the first wire sent, but after that he showed no emotion whatever, for his was not an emotional temperament. He stayed quietly with the big boss until the job was finished.

Then they went to bed and Riley slept late; but he was wakened before noon by the heavy tread of Hal Dunbar pacing in the next room of the hotel. Presently the big man came to him and talked while Riley dressed.

After breakfast, he took Riley for a short stroll outside the village.

"How's your eyes these days, Riley?" he asked. "You used to be a pretty fair sort of a shot."

"Never a hand like you with a gun," said Riley modestly, "but I'm as good as I ever was."

"You shoot well enough," Dunbar declared, "quite well enough for my purpose, Riley. Long shooting isn't your specialty, and at a short distance I think you might do very well."

He paused, and Riley waited patiently for the tale to be unfolded.

"You know," began Hal Dunbar at length, "that I've always loved a fight?"

"I know."

"And to-night I am about to fight, Riley."

"Yes?"

"But for a great prize. For the woman I love!"

"So you're going to fight Bull Hunter?"

"Yes."

Riley breathed deeply. "It will be the greatest fight that ever was fought in the mountains. But I hope not with guns!"

"It's to be with bare hands, Riley; and with so much at stake, I must not lose the fight. You understand?"

"You'll trick Bull Hunter?" asked Riley, and he looked down at the ground.

There was one article in Riley's creed, and that was fairness in fighting.

"I'll fight him fairly and squarely," said Dunbar, "and I ought to beat him with fists and hands. He's strong, but I'm still stronger, I think. Besides, I know boxing and wrestling, and he doesn't. It's a finish fight. If I down him I'll kill him with my hands. If he downs me he'll finish me the same way. But even if he leaves me dead on the ground, he must not win the fight!"

He turned and clutched the arms of his companion as he spoke.

"But how the devil——" began Riley.

"Listen to me," said Hal Dunbar. "I love that

girl in a way you can't understand. I've loved her
so long that the thought of her is in my brain and
my blood—part of me. No matter to whom she
goes, she must not go to Hunter. He ruined everything for me. If I thought that after my death he
was to have her, I tell you my ghost would come
up and haunt them. Whatever happens, no matter if
he kills me, Hunter must not win. You understand?"

Riley shook his head, bewildered.

"You fool!" gasped out Dunbar, maddened because he had to bring out the brutal truth in so many
words. "You're to be hidden near the place where
we meet, and if Hunter wins—you shoot him down.
You shoot him like a dog!"

Riley blinked. "Where do you meet?" he asked
after a pause.

Hal Dunbar sighed with relief. "You'll do it?
I thought for a minute that I was mistaken in you—
that you were weak. But you're still my right-hand
man, Riley. I'll tell you where. There's a wood
between Five Roads and Moosehorn. We're to meet
somewhere between those two towns after dark.
I'll leave early and wait for him near the trees. That
will give you a chance to stay close to the fight, and
there'll be a full moon to help you—if you have to
shoot. You understand, Riley?"

"I'll leave this afternoon and get posted?"

"Leave now. I'll follow along after a while. Go
around through Five Roads. We mustn't be seen
to ride in the same direction."

CHAPTER XXXIV

THE BATTLE

IT was thick twilight when Bull Hunter stood up from his chair in the room at Moosehorn where he and Pete Reeve had celebrated their return from outlawry to peaceful citizenship. Now the big man went to Mary Hood and took her hands.

"When a man's heart gets too full," he said quietly, "he has to get off by himself. I'm too happy, Mary, and I'm going off for a ride on Diablo all alone. I'm not even going to take The Ghost with me. Pete will take care of you."

She smiled faintly and anxiously at him as he turned to the big dog, pointed out a rug in the corner of the room, and commanded him to stay there until he was called away. The Ghost obeyed sulkily, dropping his huge scarred head upon his paws, and watching the master with an upward glance. Then Hunter turned at the door, gave himself a last look at Mary Hood, waved to Pete Reeve, and was gone.

The door had hardly closed when Mary Hood was beside the little gun fighter.

"Pete," she said, "there's something about to happen—something about to happen to Charlie. I feel it. I sensed it in his voice when he said he was going. It was queer, too, the way he watched the coming of the night. Pete, you must go out and follow him and see that he comes to no harm. Will you?"

The little man shook his head soberly. "If you're wrong and Bull finds that I'm following him, it'll be bad business," he declared. "He hates to be spied on, even by me."

"But I know that I'm right," she said eagerly. "I'm cold with the fear of it, Pete. Will you go?"

He rose slowly from his chair. "I'd ought to laugh at you," he answered. "But I can't. There's something spooky in the way a girl gets ideas about things she don't really know, and maybe you're right this time. Anyway, we can't take any chances. I'll saddle up the roan and follow Diablo as close as I can. But that isn't any easy job if Bull starts riding hard."

She thanked him huskily as he left, and from the window of the hotel she saw him lead out his little cow pony, swing into the saddle, and disappear instantly into the dusk.

The black horse was a glimmering phantom in the night far ahead of Pete Reeve, and he spurred hard after it. If Diablo had been extended to three quarters of his usual speed, he would have drawn out of sight at once, but to-night for some reason Bull Hunter was riding merely at a long, ranging gallop, giving the stallion his own way in the matter of taking hill and dale. Pete Reeve, by dint of spurring now and then, was able to keep barely within eyeshot of the rider before him.

It was precarious work to keep barely within view without being seen himself, and he kept his eyes riveted on the shadow in the darkness. The way was that leading straight to Five Roads, and with every mile he put behind him he became more and more convinced that the girl had been right. For

Bull Hunter did not ride in the careless fashion of one who is following a whim. He kept to a steady, purposeful gait, and the little man who trailed him began to suspect more and more definitely that there was a rendezvous ahead.

He rode a little closer now, for it was complete night, and the moon had not yet risen, though the light in the east gave promise of it. Pressing on with his eyes fastened on the form that moved before him, he swung a little from the beaten trail—the next moment the roan, putting his foot into an old squirrel hole, pitched forward on his head. Pete Reeve shot out of the saddle and landed heavily on his back.

When, after a time, he wakened from the trance, it was with the feeling that he had been asleep for endless hours, but he could tell by the moon, low in the east, that it had not been long. The poor roan had broken its leg and lay snorting and groaning. Pete put it out of its misery with a bullet, but he did not wait to remove the saddle.

A moral certainty had grown in him that Bull Hunter was indeed riding toward a rendezvous, perhaps to a danger. Otherwise, why such secrecy, such care in leaving even The Ghost behind? No doubt he could not arrive in time to ward off trouble, but if there were a fight he might come in time to help at the finish. Throwing his hat and cartridge belt away to lighten him, and carrying his naked Colt in his hand, Reeve started running down the road.

In the meantime Bull Hunter had come, at moonrise, to that clump of tall trees by the road, and he had found Hal Dunbar waiting on horseback. He halted, dismounted, led Diablo to the side of the road, and then advanced. Hal Dunbar—a mighty figure —came to meet him half way.

"Have you kept your word?" asked Hal Dunbar. "Have you come unarmed?"

"I have nothing but my bare hands," said Bull quietly. "But before we start, Dunbar, I want to make a last appeal to you. You've been——"

"You've not only played the sneak, but now are you going to play the fool, too, and maybe the coward?"

On the heels of his words he leaped at Bull Hunter. His right fist, driven with all the power of his body and of his leap, landed fair and true on the jaw of the other, such a blow as Bull Hunter had never felt before. It sent him reeling back and cast a cloud of misty darkness across his mind.

Hal Dunbar paused an instant to see the colossus drop. Yet, to his amazement, the other giant did not fall. The slight pause gave Hunter's brain a chance to clear. They rushed together, shocked, and again the heavy fists of Dunbar crushed home. This time he changed his aim, and the blows thudded against the body of Hunter.

It was like smiting ribs of steel. Hal Dunbar gave back, gasping his astonishment. Here was a man of stone indeed, and the first fear in battle that he had ever had came to the rancher. He tried again and again, every trick at his command. He hooked and swung and drove long straight rights with all the strength of his big body behind them. Half of those punches landed fairly and squarely. They shook Bull Hunter, but they did not topple him from his balance. His face was bleeding from half a dozen cuts—the flesh of his body must have been bruised purple—but still there was not the slightest faltering.

He seemed to be fighting a helpless, hopeless fight. The trained footwork of his antagonist kept him easily out of the range of his own unskillful punches, while from a distance Dunbar whipped his blows home and then danced away again.

But at the very moment when Dunbar seemed to have victory in the hollow of his hand, with only time as the question, his terror began to become blind panic, for the strength and endurance of Hunter were incredible. Blows that should have felled an ox glanced harmlessly from him.

Finally a blow landed squarely. It was not a powerful blow, but it sent a jar up the arm of Hunter, and the new sensation excited him. He was a new man. He came in with a low shout, rushing eagerly, no longer dull-eyed, but keenly aggressive. He became lighter on his feet, infinitely swifter of hand. At the very time that Dunbar was beating him he had been studying the methods of the tall fellow, and now he used them himself.

Then it became impossible to avoid him altogether. For all his lightness of footwork, Dunbar found terrific punches crashing through his guard. He himself was fighting like a madman, striking three times to every once for Hunter; his arms were growing weary, his guard lowering—and then like a flash, striking overhand, the long arm of Hunter shot across, and his right fist met the jaw of Dunbar. The latter dropped as though hit by a club, and Hunter leaned over him.

In the shadow of the trees Riley raised his revolver, but Hunter was saying: "Dunbar, call this the end. You're growing tired. You're getting weak. I can feel it. Don't force this on. You've fought hard. You've cut me to pieces, but now you're done, and I've no malice."

He stopped. Hal Dunbar had worked himself to his knees, looking up with a bleeding face at his conqueror. As he kneeled there, his hand closed on a huge, knotted branch of a tree, torn off in some storm by wind or lightning or both, and flung here beside the road.

The feel of the wood sent a thrill of new and savage hope through him. Vaguely he realized, not that his enemy had spared him when he might have finished the battle with a helpless foe, but simply that he was alive and that a chance to kill had been thrust into his hand. He leaped from his knees straight at Hunter, swung the branch, and struck.

The first blow beat down the arms which Hunter had raised to guard his head and struck him glancingly, but the second landed heavily, and Hunter crumpled on the ground in a shapeless heap. Hal Dunbar, with savage joy, caught him by the shoulder and wrenched him back. He laid his hand on the heart. It beat steadily but feebly, and Dunbar, gone mad with the battle, swung up the club for the finishing blow.

He was stopped by a cold, sharp voice from the wood which he hardly recognized as the voice of Riley.

"If you hit him again with that, I'll shoot you full of holes."

The amazement turned his blood to ice. He turned, gaping, and there came little Riley, walking from the shadow of the wood with the revolver leveled.

"I couldn't stand the gaff," said Riley calmly. "All the time you were fighting, I watched, and when I seen Hunter knock you down I pulled the gun, to kill him. But he let you get up, and then you whale him with a club and want to brain him after you've knocked him cold. Listen, Dunbar, I'm through with you. I ain't a saint, but neither am I skunk. I'm through with you, and so will every other decent man be some of these days. Step back from Hunter or I'll kill you."

The giant obeyed, his face working, unable to speak. The little man followed, making savage gestures with his weapon.

"You ain't worthy of touching his hand," said Riley slowly. "You ain't as good as the dirt he walks on. Now get on your hoss and ride!" He raised his hand: "Listen!"

Far off down the road they heard a voice.

"Bull! Oh, Bull Hunter!"

"It's Pete Reeve," said Riley. "He must of guessed at some dirty work. Get on your hoss and ride one way, and I'll get on mine and ride another. It won't do much good for either of us to be found here by Pete Reeve."

"Riley," said Hal Dunbar, "the day will come when you'll drag yourself on your knees to me, and I'll kick you away."

"Maybe, but it ain't come yet. What I'm thinking about just now is that being so wise as you and me have been, Dunbar, don't always pay. Here's a simple gent lying here stunned. Well, it ain't the first time that he's beat the both of us. He's lying there knocked cold, but he'll be found by a partner, Pete Reeve, and he'll be brought back to Moosehorn, and he'll marry the prettiest girl we ever seen. And how does he get all this? Just by being simple, Hal, and honest. Which, God help our souls, we ain't either of them things. Now get out of my sight!"

Whether he fled from his own shame or remorse, or was moved by the threat of his companion, or dreaded the voice of Pete Reeve coming down the road, Hal Dunbar turned his horse and galloped away. Riley returned to his covert in the woods until he saw Pete Reeve come and bend over the fallen man. When he heard Bull Hunter sigh, Riley turned and slipped away into the night. He had lived one perfect day.

THE END

THE WHITE WOLF

MAX BRAND

"Brand is a topnotcher!"
—*New York Times*

Tucker Crosden breeds his dogs to be champions. Yet even by the frontiersman's brutal standards, the bull terrier called White Wolf is special. With teeth bared and hackles raised, White Wolf can brave any challenge the wilderness throws in his path. And Crosden has great plans for the dog until it gives in to the blood-hungry laws of nature. But Crosden never reckons that his prize animal will run at the head of a wolf pack one day—or that a trick of fate will throw them together in a desperate battle to the death.

_3870-6 $4.50 US/$5.50 CAN

RIP-ROARIN' ACTION AND ADVENTURE BY THE WORLD'S MOST CELEBRATED WESTERN WRITER!

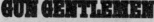

Renowned throughout the Old West, Lucky Bill has the reputation of a natural battler. Yet he is no remorseless killer. He only outdraws any gunslinger crazy enough to pull a six-shooter first. Then Bill finds himself on the wrong side of the law, and plenty of greenhorns and gringos set their sights on collecting the price on his head. But Bill refuses to turn tail and run. He swears he'll clear his name and live a free man before he'll be hunted down and trapped like an animal.

_3937-0 $4.50 US/$5.50 CAN

Dorchester Publishing Co., Inc.
65 Commerce Road
Stamford, CT 06902

Please add $1.75 for shipping and handling for the first book and $.50 for each book thereafter. NY, NYC, PA and CT residents, please add appropriate sales tax. No cash, stamps, or C.O.D.s. All orders shipped within 6 weeks via postal service book rate. Canadian orders require $2.00 extra postage and must be paid in U.S. dollars through a U.S. banking facility.

Name _____

Address _____

City _____ State _____ Zip _____

I have enclosed $_____ in payment for the checked book(s).
Payment <u>must</u> accompany all orders.☐ Please send a free catalog.

RONICKY DOONE'S TREASURE

"Brand is a topnotcher!"
—New York Times

A horsebreaker, mischief-maker, and adventurer by instinct, Ronicky Doone dares every gunman in the West to outdraw him—and he always wins. But nothing prepares him for the likes of Jack Moon and his wild bunch. Hunting down a fortune in hidden loot, the desperadoes swear to string up or shoot down anyone who stands in their way. When Doone crosses their path, he needs a shootist's skill and a gambler's luck to survive, and if that isn't enough, his only reward will be a pine box.

__3748-3 $3.99 US/$4.99 CAN

TIMBAL GULCH TRAIL

"Brand is a topnotcher!"
—*New York Times*

Les Burchard owns the local gambling palace, half the town, and most of the surrounding territory, and Walt Devon's thousand-acre ranch will make him king of the land. The trouble is, Devon doesn't want to sell. In a ruthless bid to claim the spread, Burchard tries everything from poker to murder. But Walt Devon is a betting man by nature, even when the stakes are his life. The way Devon figures, the odds are stacked against him, so he can either die alone or take his enemy to the grave with him.

_3828-5 $4.50 US/$5.50 CAN

THE MOUNTAIN FUGITIVE

First Time In Paperback!

"Brand is a topnotcher!"
—*New York Times*

A wild youth, Lee Porfilo is always in trouble. If he isn't knocking someone down, he is ready to battle any cowpoke who comes along. But a penniless brawler can't stand up to the power of rich ranchers, and the Chase brothers will do whatever it takes to defeat Lee—even frame him for murder.

Porfilo has to choose between the hangman's noose and a desperate bid to prove his innocence. His every move dogged by lawmen and bounty hunters, he flees into the wilderness. But a man can't run forever, and Lee Profilo would rather die facing his enemies head on than live as an outlaw and coward.

_3574-X $3.99 US/$4.99 CAN

Dorchester Publishing Co., Inc.
65 Commerce Road
Stamford, CT 06902

Please add $1.75 for shipping and handling for the first book and $.50 for each book thereafter. NY, NYC, PA and CT residents, please add appropriate sales tax. No cash, stamps, or C.O.D.s. All orders shipped within 6 weeks via postal service book rate. Canadian orders require $2.00 extra postage and must be paid in U.S. dollars through a U.S. banking facility.

Name_____
Address_____
City _____ State_____Zip_____
I have enclosed $_____in payment for the checked book(s).
Payment <u>must</u> accompany all orders.☐ Please send a free catalog.